A Jack Hadley Mystery

SHOOTING ANGELS

John Selby

~~~~~~~~~~~~~~~~~~~~

Copyright 2018 by John Selby

Published by the WizeWell Media Group
All Rights Reserved

ISBN: 978-1522745044

LIMITED EDITION B5

reg. WGA-W 2014-2018

For film-rights information contact Birgitta Steiner:
birgitta2424@gmail.com

~~~~~~~~~~~~~~~~~~~~~~~~~~~~

b1562397x

they have been granted
the power to seek an
opening to freedom
and leap through it

but having seen the angel of light
they shall no longer praise us –
clinging as we do
to our quagmire past
of decomposed tradition
which labeled mystics as barbarians
and failed to heed the prophets

but they have been
granted the power
to seek an opening
into the light
... and leap

B Budd Smith / Mind Dance

~ ~ ~ ~ ~ ~ ~ ~ ~ ~ ~ ~ ~ ~

1

The bedroom phone started ringing way past midnight and woke Ty Hadley up with a jolt. Usually a call that late meant he had to put on his part-time badge and go deal with yet another bothersome alcohol-induced situation somewhere in the valley – but this time it was his son Jon who was calling from that seminary he'd recently moved to, up north of San Francisco somewhere in Marin.

"Hey Dad."

"Jonathan – you know what time it is?"

"Sorry – you won't believe what just happened."

Still half asleep, Ty shifted slightly into humor mode. "Don't tell me you've finally found Jesus?"

"This isn't funny – they're claiming I'm the one who shot him."

"Shot who – Jesus?"

"Well, not exactly."

"I'm hardly awake, talk straight to me."

"Okay. My friend Paul, he's dead. Somebody shot him right through the head."

"That's fucked."

"And I need your help up here right away. Bring your badge. The drive'll take about six hours."

"Hold on – just exactly where are you?"

"Uhm – San Anselmo jail."

"Not good."

"Head north all the way up and through the City and across Golden Gate bridge, then on up ten miles, San Rafael exit, head west five miles. Police station is just off Sir Francis Drake, right in town on your left."

"But come clean with me – if you shot this guy I can't come try to get you off, you know that."

"Fuck – of course I didn't do it," Jon reacted. "He was my best friend."

"So how come they think you did the deed?"

"You remember that .22 long-nose pistol you gave me a while back for Christmas?"

"Bit pricey but nice piece."

"That's what he was shot with. They caught me by the body with the gun in my hand."

"So – do you know who did the shooting?"

"Nobody would shoot Paul."

"You have any legal help yet?"

"No, I just now got hauled in."

"Okay, I'll be up there first thing in the morning. Don't talk to nobody."

"Right. Hey. Thanks."

"That's what dads are for. Just as long as you didn't shoot him."

"Honest to God."

"Alright then. Good enough for me."

2

Just six hours earlier, as his diary shows, Jon Hadley had been a free man driving over-fast to an important meeting, speeding south on Sir Francis Drake Drive through Mill Valley to catch the freeway to Sausalito, then over the big bridge at the tip of Sausalito Bay and down to the parking lot at the harbor.

A middle-aged friend of Jonathan's named Alan Watts owned a big old houseboat called the *Vallejo*, a forty-foot two-decker ferry that had once plied the local waters of San Francisco Bay. The converted houseboat was now moored permanently in Sausalito's small-boat harbor, along with about thirty other floating homes. On that moonlit night of January 11, 1969, Jonathan was hurrying to the houseboat to discuss an unexpected dilemma – his best friend at the seminary had taken LSD and (almost but not quite) somehow turned into a walking-talking and highly-charismatic Jesus figure on campus – and now in the local media.

Knowing he was late, Jon half-ran from the parking lot down a series of floating docks to the slightly-rocking *Vallejo*. The wind was cold and salty on his lips, the moon hidden behind Sausalito's jutting hill, stars sharp in the sky. Walking the wobbly gang-plank onto the house boat, Jon heard vague fragments of a blues song Jerry Garcia was singing on a stereo somewhere nearby.

Just then he heard a short outburst of laughter coming from the houseboat – and walked the plank onboard.

Crossing the outside deck and pushing open the door into the big room, he looked around at about twenty people, most of whom were sitting atop throw pillows on the floor. He noticed several seminary friends and a dozen members of Alan's inner circle – but Alan hadn't invited any press to this meeting, not even the *Oracle* reporter from Berkeley who'd broken Paul's transformation story three days ago.

As usual, Alan was on his own pillow in front – a short skinny hipster philosopher, well-known for mystic psychology books and college lectures that the younger generation eagerly gobbled up. "I mean seriously," he was saying in his British accent as Jonathan entered, "our society has always been controlled by a political, religious, or social boss of some kind. Now comes this fellow Paul, who's definitely attained at least temporary status as a spiritual presence – but hear me on this. Paul must not be pushed into becoming yet another new boss-man."

Alan spied Jonathan standing in back. "Oh, there you are. Where's Paul, we're all set – isn't he with you?"

"Paul decided not to come," Jon told him.

"But you were supposed to bring him – how are we going to help the man if he doesn't even show up?"

"Alan," Jon said impatiently, his upset mood making his voice edgy, "if Spirit's really speaking through Paul like you say, he can choose for himself what to do and when he needs help. He's totally down tonight and doesn't want to talk to anyone."

"Oh. I see." Alan eyed Jonathan's terse expression with concern. "Yes, you're right, he's certainly free to do what he wants. I could tell from his talk today that he's tapping inspiration from far beyond – I was hoping we could go even deeper with him tonight. But reality holds sway as usual. Have a seat, let's tune in."

Jon sat slouched on a pillow. A few moments went by in Zen silence – no sounds but the gently lapping of tiny waves against the old wooden hull, and the flapping of a flag somewhere nearby in the breeze. Then somebody sneezed. Jon tried to watch his breathing, quiet his thoughts and slip into that special place that Alan was teaching him to enter – but his emotions were a wreck and his breathing tight.

Alan spoke again: "Okay, so what I feel is this," he said to the group in his emphatic teacher tone. "For several days now, Paul has been in direct communion with that ego-less Taoist realm within which all is being revealed, he's been graciously communicating to us from that expanded spiritual vista. Since he isn't here to share with us tonight, let's relax, open up our hearts, shush our egos and join him in this universal realm of the organic unified whole. Experience an effortless expansion of your being with each new spontaneous breath."

During several of his own breath cycles, Alan looked into the apt gaze of his followers, then tuned inward again: "Something momentous is definitely happening – and we must support Paul, become an awakened community, help him birth not a new religious or political movement, but a pure spontaneous awakening – a new social creation that's spiritually guided rather than politically driven. This is what Jesus originally taught. Perhaps right now in this moment we're participating in that long-awaited holy birth of a truly awakened heart-centered society."

"But wait, Alan," someone in the front spoke up. "You're talking as usual nice and pretty but you're avoiding the main issue with Paul. He attained his high spiritual state by taking a psychedelic. Does this mean everybody needs to drop acid?"

"No – Paul said over and over the last few days that we need to do nothing, just trust and devoutly listen to our own inner voice, effortlessly allow this new reality to unfold without ego manipulation. Trust is the word for tonight. Let's relax our minds, go beyond words into meditation. Sandy, play us some flute, sooth our souls."

"But Alan," an elderly woman in rather elegant attire said from her folding chair by the side wall. "Please be pragmatic for just one moment. The reality is that Paul will draw more and more crowds if he continues tomorrow with his admittedly Christ-like teachings. This could become exponential, sweep the country, the whole world. But I must ask you all – what about this growing media frenzy that wants to gobble Paul up – is it really what Paul needs right now?"

"Doris, please. Paul's flow is simply happening. Everyone's been praying for twenty centuries for Jesus to return. What if we're living right now in the eternal moment of emerging spirit? Paul was saying to us just hours ago, and the great masters have always advised – we must consciously quiet our minds, let go of our worries and participate in the greater unfolding. Let's fully trust our higher selves and we commune with our source. Flute please."

3

At around ten everyone departed the ferryboat except Jonathan. Alan led him up rickety stairs to the small enclosed captain's room where Alan maintained his private consultation space.

"So," he said, nailing Jon with an intense look. "Your aura's a mess − tell me what happened tonight with Paul. He seemed just fine at his afternoon talk in the meadow. Remarkable in fact."

"He totally crashed during dinner, drank wine and then went mute, angry, caught up in some old negative emotion. I'm getting worried, Alan − maybe he needs professional help. Julia's way beyond her limits with him. Me too."

"Okay then. Tomorrow morning first thing I'll cancel my lecture in the City, come and talk with him, maybe take him up to my cabin. It must be bizarre for his unformed ego, tapping into such a pristine level of realization. How are you holding up?"

"Seriously shaky − getting by."

Alan nodded, relaxed on the sofa. "Just remember to stay centered in your breathing − some new spiritual beast is being born and we're all still caught up blindly inside its great dark rumbling belly."

"Okay, whatever," Jon said back to Alan's flow of guru advice. "I need to get back."

"Paul's wife Julia. Beautiful girl. You and her, is something going on? This situation could turn explosive. Paul the jealous husband could come unhinged."

"Non-issue," Jon reacted. "They hadn't made love for five months, Paul was gone every day till late at night, in the Seminary library reading Gnostic manuscripts."

"Which ones?"

"Lately the ones talking about psilocybin mushroom rites in Gnostic initiation ceremonies. That's what provoked him to try LSD."

"By the way, two CIA guys came by."

Jonathan tensed. "Not good."

"Like I told you, Tim has played them for fools for years now, but something's gone sour and he needs a place to retreat. You come from that big ranch way out in nowhere, what's the chance he could disappear there for a week or two?"

"My dad would flip."

"You told me he was fairly hip for a cowboy."

"He's doing his best these last few months to understand me – but he's a deputy sheriff down there and that means that Leary and my Dad – no way. Look, I need to get back to Paul."

"They were asking about you too."

Jon froze. "What about?"

"The Sandoz thing we talked about before, that's what they're focused on."

"They have zero proof I took the stuff, there were a dozen people back at the Institute who could have stolen those bottles."

"Two quarts of pure LSD is enough to get five million people blasted. That's crazy power – please, Jon, let me help on this. Don't mess with the CIA."

"If there are any magic power jars around, they're well stashed and out of circulation. Look, I gotta run."

"Did you hear," Alan went on, "that the Institute was suddenly shut down last week?"

"No – I cut communication when I left."

"I just talked with Humphry, he's very upset as you might imagine, he's maybe heading back in Canada."

"Good riddance."

"Please, Humphry did his absolute best with you, considering the circumstances when you departed. He's a great man and he deserves your reverence. By the way, how's your memory of all that?"

"Fucking foggy as usual."

"Well then. Let's return to this when we get Paul a bit more stable. I'll be at your cottage around nine. Take care of our boy. You taken any acid lately?"

"Life's intense enough right now without it. I'm not a philosopher looking for any more psychedelic explosions."

"You still managing the seminary scene?"

"Better than being in 'Nam but Christian history just gets darker the deeper I look. Like Paul was saying today, it's way too easy for the light to go black and with Nixon getting inaugurated next week, things could go totally dark."

"Well I'm here for you, you know that. Let me know where I can help. Now go on home and take special care of our Paul."

4

Around 11:20, according to the journal notes he took a week afterwards, Jonathan approached the entrance gate leading into the seminary. The whole hill-top campus was surrounded by a high stone wall with only this opening for cars to enter. For the fist time in seminary history, provoked by the sudden situation of Paul and his riff-raff followers, the Administration had posted a security man at the gate to ID everybody entering seminary property – but after 11 there was no guard.

Jon drove on through the gate, up along redwood trees past dorm buildings and the three stone mock-castle edifices housing administration, library and lecture halls – then up the final steep climb to the top of Holy Hill where, fifty years ago, two dozen small cottages had been built atop Holy Hill for married students – two humble rows of houses with rustic paths meandering among redwoods on each side of the sloping hill.

Jon parked and walked down to the left, past the first row of cottages toward his own domicile in the second row. He pushed away the hope that Julia would surprise him in his bed as she had several times recently. Luckily Paul was a deep sleeper. Jon hoped she'd been able to ease Paul out of the mood that had come over him a few hours before. They might both be asleep for the night. This whole thing had become so crazy, out of hand, beyond anything Jon could have imagined –

Caught up in a cacophony of confused thoughts, Jon saw lights still on next door in Paul's living room. His stomach tensed, he considered knocking to see how they were doing – and it was just at that moment that a single jolting gunshot pierced the peace of Holy Hill.

Jonathan stopped dead in his tracks, not believing his ears. The sudden memory of handing Julia his .22 pistol two afternoons ago filled his mind – he'd almost certainly just heard that same pistol being discharged in Paul's cottage. Apprehension grabbed at his breathing, he almost turned to run like hell back up the path to his car, expecting Paul to swing open the front door of his cottage and come out shooting at Jon after having killed Julia –

But he didn't run nor did Paul open the front door. After maybe ten seconds of blank hesitation, Jon's body started moving again on its own, walking on down the path, forcing him to approach Paul's door. The sound of his own breathing was loud and raw in his ears as he made it to the front porch of the cabin, then stood silently a moment at the door –

Did he hear sounds of somebody going out the other entrance down into the woods? Yes – that was the back door closing. Jon pounded on the front door hard with his knuckles three times – then without waiting he tried the knob. It turned and the door opened and he half-stumbled into the small living room of the cottage.

Even before he could shout for Julia he saw Paul there, sitting comfortably in his recliner chair, quiet and at peace – with his eyes staring off into blank space. There was just the one lamp giving light to the room and at first

Jon failed to notice the small dark hole in the center of Paul's forehead.

"Paul – what's up?" he managed to mutter.

Then he saw the pistol on the floor between him and Paul. Without thinking he reached down and grabbed the gun – just in time to straighten up and turn at the sound of hurried footsteps coming down into the cottage through the front door.

Julia stood there for one short eternal moment staring at her dead husband, then staring at the very much still-alive Jon Hadley – standing there with the pistol in his hand that must have just killed her husband.

She did what anybody would – gaping at the corpse and seeing the bullet hole, she screamed bloody murder and went running back out of the house in a freaked-out panic.

5

Bad news spreads fast – horror attracts. It seemed like the whole campus had almost instantly congregated atop Holy Hill in the misty chill of midnight. Police came and pushed them back behind quickly-tied-off police ribbon. No one talked much to each other – what was there to say after you heard the basic news:

"Hey – what happened?"

"Somebody just shot Paul Jacobs. Dead."

"But – nobody would do that."

"They have Jon Hadley inside, it seems he did it. You know Jonathan?"

"We do German Theology together, Tuesday and Thursday. He's best friends with Paul."

"Well they found him with a pistol in his hand standing over the body."

"You're sure?"

"It's what I heard."

"I don't believe it."

"Ask anybody."

A slender strong-looking woman of about thirty-five was walking fast down the dimly-lit redwood path from the parking lot. All eyes looked to her – she had a pistol on her hip. Her shoulder-length red hair was tied back behind her head with a rubber band. She wasn't dressed like a cop but she walked like a cop. Pushing impatiently through the small crowd, she went across the lawn to the cottage and rapped on the closed door – which opened and admitted her, then closed again.

The living room was dimly lit. Forensics hadn't arrived yet but there was Dr. Franklin, just standing upright from where the body was sitting rather casually in an easy chair. The medics people must have come and gone – it had taken Kate over half an hour to get here.

She saw immediately the wound to the forehead, so symmetrical in its positioning that it looked staged – but it wasn't. She'd seen plenty of entry holes; this one would probably be a .22 from about five to eight feet, not a hollow-nose because it was a very clean entry, smaller than a dime with the blood darkening already. She had no interest in seeing the back of the head, if indeed such a low caliber would have made it all the way through.

On the couch was a young man, hand-cuffed. On the coffee table was a pistol – .22 Colt – in a plastic bag. Sergeant Walkins had his own pistol out. "Put that away, he's not going anywhere," Kate said. "What you got?"

"Deceased is Paul Jacobs."

"I recognize him. He's their Jesus."

"The deceased's wife was a couple of cottages up and to the left. She heard a shot, jumped up and went running down here to her house, two minutes at most – came in and found yours truly there, Jon Hadley, standing about where you're standing, holding that pistol in his hand. She screamed when she saw her husband there – then ran off to the neighbor where she is now. The neighbor called 911. Right around then another seminary student, Keith Oberman, came down here to see what all the shooting and screaming was about – and found our boy there, sitting cross-legged on the rug, still holding the gun. We arrived six minutes later."

Kate took all this in without interrupting. Walkins was a good cop, wasted in this small town department – just like her. She nodded to him, then looked to the still-alive younger man in the room. He was staring into space, not hardly there. She walked over to him.

"Jon," she said. He looked up. "That's your friend there," she said evenly to him. "I was on campus this weekend – you were at his side wherever he went. Buddies. What was the argument, what happened?"

Still he said nothing.

"Tell me, why'd you do it, son?"

He blinked, his emotions in ragged condition.

"Why did you come here to see Paul tonight?" she pushed him to provoke a confession.

He looked listlessly over at his dead friend. He looked back at the lady cop with the pony tail. "Take these off – I didn't shoot Paul, are you crazy?"

"People found you holding the gun."

"I came back from a meeting, I was fifty feet away, I heard the shot, I started running and banged the door open and there he was, just like he is now."

"And the gun?"

"I saw it on the floor. It was mine."

"What?"

"I'd loaned it to Julia a couple of days ago."

"Why would you do that?"

"You must know – there had been threats."

"Yes, I heard," she admitted.

"At first I didn't believe my eyes – that hole in his head is so small, and he looked just asleep. But his eyes … I guess that's when I picked up the pistol. Then Julia came running in and screamed – where is she now?"

"You could have run, right at that point."

"Run from what?"

"You shot him. You shot your friend. Why?"

Again he went silent, staring at her. Nasty memories came flashing into her mind of how she'd lost her job in the city because of this same sort of situation – she felt the sweat break out down her spine. Evidence showed this kid had killed somebody. She could tell instantly by the look in his eyes that he hadn't.

And so the murder scene continued apace for another twenty minutes – cops inside with the body and the accused killer, small crowd outside unable to do anything but wait. Three gruff guys in suits came huffing along the path with suitcases of equipment – fingerprint team, somebody said. Then the hand-cuffed prisoner was led away, the body was taken off in a bag and Miss Ponytail went up to a nearby cottage to talk with the deceased's wife. The cottage where the shooting had happened was locked up and taped off, and the police dispersed the chilled knot of students.

"Hey, it's over, go on home now," Sergeant Walkins ordered them in a tired voice.

As the crowd dispersed, a solitary young man of considerable girth, with a baseball cap pulled down low over his eyes, remained standing in the shadows observing the proceedings from a distance. Stuart Wilson was well-known on campus as part of the fringe group with over-keen interest in things mystic but very little interest in the pragmatic side of the ministry. He was a long-time friend of the deceased, they'd been students at NYU and, a bit later, had come out west together. Stuart also knew the accused – but he preferred not to be visually associated by the police with either.

A few minutes earlier he'd sent his wife to the cottage Paul's wife was in retreat. His instructions to Dana were to invite Julia to spend the night with them in their cottage. Now, as planned, the two young women were emerging, walking together down the vaguely-lit path. They went right past without seeing him, and disappeared into his cottage.

A few moments later his friend Reggie found him. They'd driven back from the Watts houseboat in separate cars. Reggie Davis was a black man dressed in black, hard to see and light-footed as well. He came right up on Stuart before being noticed.

"Damn, Reggie, don't sneak around here like that," Stuart growled, his nasal Long Island accent still dominant. "Good way to get yourself shot."

"All of this – fuckin' insane," Reggie muttered right back, his own accent originating no farther from the scene than Oakland.

"Yeah, Paul suddenly gone and Jon down – major train wreck for us but we'll make do, no cause for alarm."

"Get real, Stu, this ain't some drama in our heads, man – I mean Paul's been fuckin' murdered!" Reggie was twenty-three, skinny and street-wise, way smarter than his diction would imply, recently graduated cum laude from Berkeley while also a silent member of the Black Panthers over in Oakland. Stuart scowled at him impatiently. "Hey, you need to cool it, get a grip," he ordered.

Reggie looked ready to break down and cry out with his blownaway anguish over the murder. "Gimme a break, this is real, I mean don't you have any heart at all?"

"Now's not the time to go soft."

"Well you tell me who shot him – Jonathan didn't do it, I know he didn't."

"How do you know – because perhaps you hurried back here and shot him yourself?"

"Man you're weird, you know that? I went right back to my room and rolled a joint. Jon obviously just came home and stopped by Paul's and found him dead – I mean they were tight."

"Keep your voice down," Stu ordered quietly. "If Jon didn't shoot Paul then somebody else, maybe right now within hearing distance, did the shooting. Therefore it's not cool, you hear me, to blow your cool – or you might just get yourself a bullet in your head too. Listen to me. Breathe. Focus."

Stu turned away from the slight breeze blowing up from the redwood stand that separated the cottages from the rest of the seminary buildings down below. He lit a wooden match on his Levi's and went through his momentary ritual of lighting a cigarette, inhaling deeply, then slowly exhaling. "So Jon's in jail – and with Paul down we're cut off," he muttered under his breath, mostly to himself. "I need to check out Julia."

"She shot Paul?"

"Could be – he was rough sometimes with her, back in New York, get drinking and bang her around. And Jon's been banging her for weeks now."

"But still that doesn't add up to murder."

"Ask any cop, it's money or sex. Anyway there's a good chance she knows where the stuff's been stashed. Come with me, take Dana for a walk somewhere, give me time to dig into Julia. Where's Doug, you seen Doug around?"

"No, no Doug."

"Damn."

6

Around half past midnight, twenty fast-driving minutes after receiving a phone call informing him of the seminary shooting, Alan Watts came storming into the San Anselmo police station.

Detective Kate Douglas, having finally settled her prisoner into a cell and phoned to make sure the victim's body was on ice at the morgue, was sitting at her typewriter in her office making preliminary notes. Hearing a commotion down the hall, she went to see what the problem was.

"... I told you, my name is Alan Watts and I demand access to Jonathan Hadley," a short tense man was shouting at the night clerk. "This is preposterous, he's no more a murderer than I am."

Kate walked up behind the short fellow. "That remains to be seen," she said.

He spun around at her. "Why hasn't Jon even been given his usual phone call?' he demanded.

"Calm yourself, sir. He has made his call."

"He would have phoned me but he didn't. I had to get the information through the grapevine."

"He phoned his father."

"But – I'm the one who can help him."

"I attended a lecture of yours a few weeks ago, Mr. Watts, and I'm sure you're competent in arguing theological issues, but what Jon Hadley needs is a damn good lawyer – and that can wait till tomorrow."

Alan took in the person confronting him. She was a bit taller than himself, her wild head of red curly hair barely contained with a rubber band, blouse and slacks unable to hide a quite enticing physical presence. "Well, and just who are you?" he asked her.

"I am Detective Douglas."

"Cops don't come in your size. You're beautiful."

"That is irrelevant, Mr. Watts."

"Call me Alan."

"What can I do for you, sir? It's late."

"I insist on talking with Jon."

"Come back tomorrow."

"I know the finest lawyers in California – don't throw police tricks at me. I must talk with Jon tonight, that's why I drove all the way up here."

"I can tell that you usually get everything you want, Mr. Watts, but not with me. The events of the evening have overwhelmed the boy. Are you a relative or a legal representative of the prisoner?"

"Uhm – no."

"Then return in the morning."

"But what about Paul – his death is an absolute tragedy, you must realize that."

"Any violent death is a tragedy," she reposted. "But yes, especially after what's been happening the last few days with Paul, everything he shared with us before he died, this is difficult to come to terms with."

"You went to one of his talks?"

"Most of them. It was my assignment to manage the gatherings peacefully. I admit I was moved by the young man's words. Now he's dead and just – gone."

"You saw him dead?"

"Hole in the head. Instant lights-out."

Alan stood there a moment with tears suddenly blurring his vision. "Yes, well," he muttered. "But you can't think that Jon actually shot him – where's the evidence? I demand that you release him this instant."

She sighed. "Mister Watts, you can trust me," she said honestly. "I'll do my very best to find out who murdered Paul Jacobs. Now I'm exhausted and shall say good night."

She turned and walked back down the hallway to her office. Alan watched until she disappeared, then turned on booted heel and walked out of the building, trying to grasp the larger truth of Paul Jacobs being dead and gone, so suddenly –

He stood outside under the moon for a long moment, feeling shaky right down to his bones. What's going on here, he beseeched the universe – what's happening to us?

Back inside, Kate was feeling similar emotions as she set up an army cot over in the corner of her office, took off her shoes, pulled a couple of blankets over her and fell immediately asleep.

Five hours later Detective Kate Douglas was upright again, sitting alone in her office holding a cup of black coffee, pulling her scattered thoughts together before going out to give a press report and then head back to the scene of the crime to continue with interviewing. The San Anselmo Police Department was both underfunded and understaffed – unprepared to handle the events leading up to and following this shooting atop Holy Hill. She'd of course done everything according to the book, knowing all too well she couldn't afford another procedural disaster on her record.

Someone had been knocking on her door for quite some time before she became cognizant of the pounding. She opened her eyes and stared at the space inside the room without really seeing it. Why weren't they using the intercom, for Christ's sake!

"I'll be out in two," she shouted vaguely back at the recurrent pounding.

Her office door opened – it was Lorrie. "Sorry, but I think you will want to meet with this man right now," she said, and stepped aside as a tall hungry-looking middle-aged guy in faded Levi's with realistic sweat-stained cowboy hat came walking in, wearing a pair of well-worn hand-stitched cowboy boots.

Kate looked up at his gaunt handsome presence and met unexpectedly-blue eyes, set deep in his suntanned face. "So," she muttered, thinking again of the news crews outside impatiently awaiting her statement, "how'd you get through the pandemonium out there?"

"I pushed, they gave."

He flashed his shield at her with a nonchalant hand-move. She paused to inspect it: San Luis Obispo Deputy Sheriff.

"You're holding Jon Hadley – he's my son," he told her outright.

"Ah – uhm. Oh, I see," she said slowly.

"Hey, you okay?" he asked her.

"What? Yes. Have a seat. It's been an all-nighter."

"Same here."

"You drove all the way up from SLO?"

"Yep."

They eyed each other. He saw a good looking but hard-nosed woman, a bit younger than himself, naturally well-preserved, not too skinny, not too fat – with eyes that missed not a thing, including his glances at her twin harnessed breasts she always wished were smaller and attracted less attention.

"That badge won't do you any good up here. Your boy's asleep down the hall, no point in waking him – he was traumatized by the shooting. Swears he didn't do it."

"What do you think?"

"I think your son is in very hot water whether he did the shooting or not. You need to just walk out of here right now, head north two blocks to Jackal Street, hang a left into the Hard Egg Café. Order me an Ortega omelet, I'll be there in fifteen."

"You look like you need to crash a while before you do anything," he told her.

"Well so do you."

At that same moment atop Holy Hill, inside Jon's cottage where she'd retreated rather than staying with Dana, Julia Jacobs opened her eyes to the sound of someone breaking into the cottage through the back door she was certain she'd locked. The cottage was not her own but she knew the rooms well. Sensing trouble, she slipped out of the bed and hurried silently on bare feet into the bathroom, closed the door behind her and turned the flimsy lock.

Relative quiet reigned for a few breathless moments. Then another few moments. She'd slept as usual without clothes, and the morning air was cold on her naked skin. She began to wonder if she'd dreamed or imagined the intruder sounds. Who would be breaking into Jon's house – the murderer?

Suddenly there was sound again – this time of someone barging into the bedroom and throwing things around, opening drawers over-fast, doing other things she couldn't recognize by the sound. Then for a few moments there was silence – then footsteps coming fast toward the bathroom door.

She considered standing her ground and attempting one of the karate kicks she'd been learning. She eyed the window just as the intruder started trying to get the bathroom door open. She climbed into the tub and struggled to get the old latch open. The intruder was now crashing against the door – she screamed with all her might to make her arms force the stuck window open.

The splintering crash of the door breaking behind her came at the same time the window broke free and slid upward in its frame – just high enough for her to lunge out through the opening and crash down five feet into the branches of a winter-brittle shrub. Her long black hair got caught in it. she struggled to break free and get up onto her feet, growling and yanking her head back, ripping strands of hair from her scalp but gaining her freedom.

The one thing she didn't do, that she later wished she had as she ran like hell across the lawn, was turn her head to catch a view of the intruder in that window. She neither knew who he was nor whether he'd recognized her. Instead she went speeding away on bare feet, gasping for breath – and ran right into the innocent arms of one of the neighbors, a conservative young seminarian from Nebraska who in turn screamed bloody murder as a beautiful female apparition totally devoid of adornment grabbed at him and held tight to his body, pressing her naked abundance against him so fiercely that he came close to passing out before she pushed away from him, recovered a bit – and collapsed down cross-legged right there before him, exposed breasts rising and falling as she struggled to regain her breath …

Tyson was just saying to Kate: "Everybody seems to know you here."

She shrugged from across the café table. "I'm not the kind to snuggle alone with my coffee at home. Frank in there's a good cook. What kind of deputy sheriff are you?"

"Part time. Not my main gig."

"Which is?"

"Cattle. Alfalfa. Bunch of grapes. And you're hardly the typical small-town cop."

"Shall I take offense at that?"

"Just an observation"

"Anyway, about your boy. I got a report on that pistol already. It happens to be registered in your name."

"Gave it to him when he went off to college. You gotta have a handgun when you take off for nowhere."

"That's one attitude – look where it gets you."

"At least it wasn't him that got shot."

"Better the death penalty than a hole in the head?"

"What's happened procedure-wise?"

"He's booked on first degree – shot the guy from six feet away. Bang. Premeditated if he brought the gun."

"Look, Karen. Just – "

"Kate."

"Kate. I asked him already on the phone if he did the shooting. He said no."

She looked this big sophisticated country bruiser right back in the eye. "I asked him too," she said. "I got there forty minutes after the shooting, half an hour after another local cop first arrived — I live way up the canyon. Your boy was just sitting stunned on the sofa, staring blankly at his dead buddy. They were friends."

"That's what he told me."

"I've seen more than my share of shootings."

"In this town?"

"Until recently I was down in the City. With your boy — his answers weren't what someone says if he just shot his best friend. That's a hard tone to fake."

"Jonathan would never lie to me."

"There's a lot you don't know. Stuff's been happening up on Holy Hill these last few days, crazy stuff centered around that dead kid."

"So fill me in."

"You think you're part of this investigation?"

"I ain't going away if that's what you mean."

The radio she was packing buzzed. She reached for it on her hip, listened, mumbled — put it away. "So much for breakfast," she said. "More trouble on Holy Hill. You can tag along but keep your mouth shut and don't get in the way."

"And if I do?"

"Then you'll have no one at all on your kid's side." She eyed him, then stood up and threw down a twenty. As they walked out of the café she said quietly to him, "Between you and me — unless I bring in somebody from higher up the chain than San Anselmo, experience-wise I'm all alone on this one. You at least look like you can shoot straight and play hound-dog. Unless it's your boy who fired that shot, we still have the shooter out there."

"Got'cha."

"The DA here is a jerk, he'll go after your boy because he was caught with the murder weapon in hand.

I'm gunna prove your kid didn't do it – and get my hands around the neck of whoever did."

"You've got a lot of passion for a cop."

"This dead boy Paul," she said. "Four days ago he reportedly took some LSD and turned into a walking talking Jesus, talking from such a deep spiritual place. And almost immediately, news got out and loads of people showed up to listen to him. The seminary asked us in to keep the gatherings peaceful. I'm basically an atheist but when I heard Paul I admit, at least to you, he hit me right in the quick. And as far as I'm concerned, whoever shot him should be shot. And just now, somebody's gone and messed with his wife. My fault, I should have posted a watch up there last night."

7

She drove them fast toward the western foothills of Mount Tamalpais, passing through the quiet old town of San Anselmo and then slowing down as they approached a gated entrance where a security guard was regulating access to the campus.

"Holy Hill," she told him, "wasn't holy at all back when the seminary started in 1871 down in the City on Haight Street. This San Anselmo campus was built in 1902, converting a wooded knoll into this sleepy fairyland fortress. That high stone wall encapsulates all 34 acres of the ecclesiastic domain."

Ty looked curiously out the police-cruiser window as they stopped at the gate.

"He's with me," she said to the elderly uniformed man, and then drove on up the private road shadowed by great towering redwoods. Ty got momentarily jolted by the sight of four 50-foot-high stone turrets suddenly coming into view up ahead, attached atop three small stone castles rising several stories upward into pristine winter blueness.

The air was cool and sharp, scented with redwood sap as morning sun heated up several billion green needles. Inhaling slow and deep and pleasurably through the nose, Ty got hit with a tangy rush of olfactory pleasures that he found quite distinct from the pungent dry rangeland and lush irrigated alfalfa he was used to.

"Good air," he concluded. "I expected city stink."

"Marin has its perks."

"You wish you were still down in the smog?"

"Fuck all that," she grumbled. "I'm headed out of all this shit, not back in."

He smiled a crooked but suddenly amiable smile. "You do have a nasty barb to ya."

"Sleep deprivation – give a girl a break. So here's our situation. Whoever did the shooting was either on the outside of that wall there and climbed over, or was a seminary person already inside – or came in after 11 when the guard left for the night, which cuts the timing rather thin considering when the murder took place."

"You had a gate guard before the shooting?"

"Paul was attracting all kinds of questionable people the administration didn't want inside their walls so they hired private security – there were people all over the hill using the toilets, camping out in the woods.."

"Anybody could get over that wall with a ladder."

"That's premeditation," she retorted.

"So what's the motivation factor, who wanted that guy shot, who benefited?"

"Therein lies our investigation."

"You don't have any idea at all?" he pushed.

"Lots of people wanted the original Jesus dead. It's obvious at least one person had major reasons for nipping this new bud."

"He was that convincing?"

"It was bizarre, looking back – Paul was totally convincing, obviously enough to get himself shot dead."

"So he just got drugged up and spontaneously started spouting off like he was genuine JC calibre?"

They were approaching the top parking lot. Kate parked and cut the engine, then sat there a moment. "Your boy Jon told me last night that Paul wasn't high at all on anything after that one trip at the beginning. This LSD thing, I've seen all sorts of people under its influence lately, mostly college kids – they come across as drugged, entirely spaced cognitively but sometimes they're also, well – so lucid. Tell me, just how well do you know your boy?"

"Jonathan's always been a curious cat, brain buzzing too fast for his pants. All that genius-track stuff at school, then him going to Princeton and working at that Institute – that's where all this LSD stuff started."

"What institute?"

"All I know is what Jonathan told me – that they were discovering answers to psych questions using hypnosis and chemical additives to set the mind free, expand consciousness. The Institute was draft-deferred but Jon got in some kind of trouble there and headed for Stanford grad school but the draft board got after him."

"Well the story I've picked up is that your son encouraged the deceased to ingest a rather hefty dose of lysergic acid diethylamide. The stated intent was to stimulate spiritual awakening. Jonathan was Paul's guide or whatever during the experience from which Paul emerged as some true blue modern-day Jesus figure."

"So – the drug drove him crazy," Ty concluded.

"I wish it was that simple, but after his experience Paul seemed otherwise entirely normal and rational except when he started spontaneously speaking – then it seemed that a modern-day Jesus or Buddha was right here with us. When I took him aside, two days ago, and asked him a bunch of questions I found him rational, sharp, honest. He was just Paul – but then he'd get this particular look in his eyes ... and of course there was what he was saying. I have transcripts of almost all his talks, over 17 hours worth. Damn, I hope no one's messed with those tapes."

"It sounds like you yourself fell into the spell."

"Yes. There was some remarkably deep true voice speaking through Paul. Who's to say if he went psychotic on us or genuinely mystic – and now he's dead and forever gone and we'll never know."

"Too bad I missed the whole show."

She was looking out at the view beyond her windshield. "I love this view, that stand of ancient redwoods down around the student cottages. These old-time lodgings, isolated from the lower campus and filled these days with radical kids, look like witchy forest huts."

"You sound like you kind'a like them."

"I like what they're interested in, yeah. I have a good ear and I get around the neighborhood quite a lot, that's my life right now – there's something intense happening and Paul was the height of that intensity."

Without saying more, she got out of the car. Ty followed suit, stalking along with his long strides beside her, alert, she noticed, like some buck walking into a clearing. She spied a uniform standing by one of the cottages and walked in that direction.

"Must have scared the regular seminary people," Ty was saying, "suddenly having a new JC appearing live in technicolor."

"The Seminary panicked when the local papers picked up the story, day before yesterday and students from Berkeley and the city got word that Jesus had come to Holy Hill. Yesterday I watched the crowd swell bigger by the hour. Then Paul and his wife decided to retreat for dinner and the Seminary chased the crowd out."

"That's when the shooting happened?"

"Few hours later."

Julia was curled up alone on a sofa in the living room belonging to the student she'd run into naked a while earlier. The wife of that student had given her a slip-over dress to cover her forbidden parts. She had a cup of coffee in her hands that was still half-full. Lack of sleep mixed with utter confusion had left her mind in numb mode. The sincerely-nice wife had given up trying to soothe the poor girl's nerves and was in the kitchen cooking an omelet she hoped would help Julia regain her grip on reality.

Someone was suddenly pounding on the front door. As the woman went hurrying to open it, Julia looked up vaguely at the two people entering the room. She recognized the woman but not the man – he didn't look at all like a policeman, standing there in cowboy boots politely holding his weathered straw hat to his chest.

"Hello, Julia," the woman said. "My name's Kate, remember? This is my friend Ty. He's the father of Jon Hadley."

At the mention of Jon's name, Julia's expression shifted, took form, gained a bit of brightness. "Oh – Jon's dad?"

"Please sit down," the wife of the cottage said to them. "Anyone want coffee, perhaps an omelet?"

"Coffee would be fine," Kate told her as she collapsed down into a cozy leather chair.

Ty walked over to an upright chair close to the sofa. "Actually we're hungry if there's eggs."

Julia sipped at her coffee, glanced at one and then the other of them. "Please – how is Jon?" she asked, her voice wane, "is he still being held?"

"I'm afraid so," Kate responded.

"He didn't do it," Julia said emphatically.

"I know that," Ty agreed with her.

"He must have come in just before me and picked up the pistol – please, help him."

"To help him," Kate told her, "we need help finding out who in fact did shoot your husband."

Julia stared at the woman, her expression blank.

"Who do you think did it?" Kate gently pushed.

Julia took the words in silently. Something came to mind and her breath froze. She got tears in her eyes and a moment later started crying, at first quietly, then gripped with a sudden inner horror. Kate went over and put her arm gently around her. Ty's impression of Kate rose another notch. Tough but sweet – some cop.

Coffees and omelets arrived. Ty mumbled thanks and dug in – Kate barely touched hers. The wife stood staring a few moments, then pivoted and left the room. Julia finally pulled herself together and had just one thought in her mind. "I want my house back," she said.

"Fine, we're done there."

"I want to go now," Julia insisted. "Go catch whoever broke into Jon's cottage just now, there must be fingerprints. He was violent – he must be the one."

"You were in Jonathan's house?" Ty asked.

"I slept there."

"Not at Dana's?" Kate queried.

"No, she was – Stuart tried – no way could I stay there. Jon's place was empty, I have a key. Last night it felt safe but somebody woke me this morning kicking the back door open, banging around the living room. I went out a window as he smashed the bathroom door."

"You're sure it was a man?"

"He smashed that door."

"What was he trying to find?" Kate insisted.

"I don't know. Ask Stuart, he was quizzing me. It's true, Jon had some secret – but he never told me."

"A secret someone would kill for?"

"Talk with Dana and Stuart in the cottage on the other side of mine. I was mostly on the outside of their circle but Dana had her nose in everything."

Ty was still trying to get names straight. "Dana was who you were with when you heard the shot?"

"No, I was with Lucille, up above."

"You think Dana shot Paul?" Kate pushed.

Her face clouded again. "Nobody in this whole world would kill Paul – unless …"

"Unless what?"

"Well back in New York, there were people …"

"What people?"

"I don't think Paul heard from them since we came out here. Ask Stuart, they were pals in New York. I want to go home now."

"You going to be okay on your own?"

"I – I think so."

"We'll need you to go to the station sometime today for a statement. You have a car?"

"Ours is in the shop but I have the keys to Jon's."

"You and Jonathan – you're close?" Kate asked.

"We were – yes. Recently."

"You in love with him?"

"What? Well – maybe."

"Him with you?"

" I was going to leave Paul – all last month I was trying to make the break." She stood up. "I'm itchy and sticky and dirty and tired and I want to take a bath."

Kate stood up with her. "Tonight, do you have someplace to go stay, someone you trust?"

"Not really. We've only been here a few months and I'm not as devout as these other wives."

What about staying with Dana?"

"Definitely not Dana."

Ty put his cup down, walked to the door and opened it. "I'll be moving into Jon's house for the duration," he told Julia, noting Kate's surprised glance. "You take the bedroom, I'll take the couch. What say?"

A few minutes later they walked out of the cottage and onto the path that led down to more cottages. Ty glanced around to get his bearings. "Let me get this straight," he said as they went down the path to the lower cottages. "That'll be your place on the left with the police tape. Which one is Jon's?"

"The far one, beside mine," Julia said.

"Where were you when you heard the shot?"

She paused, turned to point to one of the higher cabins. "With Lucille, up there."

"Jonathan's version of the shooting," Kate said, "is that he was coming down this path to Paul's house when he heard the gunshot. Was the door to your cottage open when you came down?"

"Uhm – no."

"Did you see anyone else on the path?"

"No – it was late."

"So you went running down into your house?"

"I don't want to go over all this again."

"You say it took about two minutes from the time you heard the shot to when you entered your cabin."

"When I heard the shot I jumped right up."

"Who was with you in the room?"

"No one. Lucille had gone to run me a bath."

"Why were you spending the night up there, we need to know the truth or we can't help Jon."

"Well in public Paul had become so godlike and wise and all the rest – but he'd always had a rough streak and for the last couple of nights, when we were gone from all the people and alone, he'd gotten, well … "

"What?"

"Unpredictable. Scary. He went off somewhere after dinner, probably drinking. Jon couldn't find him so he went to some meeting without him. I was sitting home alone – and then Paul came back around ten, acting – weird. And I reacted."

She fell silent. "What happened?" Kate asked.

"I lost my temper, I couldn't take his silent brooding. I slapped him in the face to snap him out of his trance. He grabbed me, shouted at me, hit me so hard I ran crying and got Jon's pistol from the bottom drawer in the kitchen. Standing there with the gun aimed at him – the world was suddenly just entirely insane. I screamed something, I don't remember what, and then threw the pistol hard at him and ran outside, sobbing all the way up to Lucille's house."

"And that was the last time you saw Paul alive?"

"Uhm – yeeah."

"Where had Jon gone that evening?" Ty asked.

"Him and Stuart, Doug and Reggie, I think they went down to a houseboat in Sausalito that a local spiritual guy owns. Paul was supposed to go also but – I wish to God he'd gone!"

"What kind of meeting?"

"Please, no more. Talk to Stuart, or Doug."

"I'll come with you, make sure everything's ready," Kate offered, then caught Ty's eye. "You want to go talk to Dana and Stuart?"

"Which house is theirs?"

Julia pointed at the cottage to the right of her own. "Don't tell her I sent you."

"Roger on that. Can you cook?"

"What – of course."

"How about the three of us having dinner tonight at Jon's cottage, help bring some normalcy to all this."

He took out his wallet and handed her two twenties. She hesitated, then took them. "What do you like, a roast, potato gratin and something, spinach salad?"

"Perfect. So Kate, are you free?"

She met his eyes evenly. "I can be."

"I'll bring the wine," he said.

Julia eyed him with the first real glimmer he'd seen in her expression since he met her. She was quite startlingly beautiful when her face lit up.

8

Dana had been up since seven when the alarm went off and Stuart grunted and got out of bed to take his shower. She fine-ground his coffee beans and had a big mug ready for him by the time he appeared in the kitchen. The special home-roast beans came regularly each month from an old girlfriend of his back in New York. Stuart was a self-appointed connoisseur – he demanded the very best. Dana herself had once been a prize worth stalking and catching two years ago. She'd been a ripe twenty-year-old beauty at NYU when he returned to grad school following his Nam stint.

He came into the kitchen and found her staring out the window across fifty feet of redwoods and undergrowth toward the cottage of Julia and Paul. Approaching her from behind, he put his arms around her. Taking both of her firm squishy breasts possessively in his stubby fingers, he enjoyed the female fullness thereof – but she wasn't in the mood, she turned and pushed him back.

He was short but she was a notch shorter, making her have to look up a bit into those same pale blue-grey eyes that had once mesmerized but now held little sway over her heart. Furthermore he'd gained ten pounds since they met and she liked men who looked slim and taut. "I'm going out for a couple hours," he told her curtly, bothered by her pushing away. "If the police come asking questions about the shooting, remember they're cops – control your tongue for a change, we don't need complications."

"Where are you going?"

"Looking for Doug. If he shows up here, try to keep him entertained till I'm back – noon or so."

"I don't want to be alone with him, I've told you," she retorted. "Maybe he's your friend but he's not mine."

"Why's everybody so down on Doug?" he reacted. "He's a winner, a real American hero. And I need him. He's key. So just humor the guy."

He spooned some Ecuadorian bitter-cacao into the coffee, then added a dollop of Vanilla-bean ice cream, stirred and sipped. "Ah," he said in his self-confident voice, "just right. Paul dead to the contrary, it's still a perfect universe."

Dana preferred the cottage when Stuart was gone. She showered, luxuriated in her soapy girl games, then put on an assortment of the flimsy clothes Stuart bought for her to wear, hoping Doug wouldn't' come by and violate her morning solitude. She was sipping a cup of strong tea when knuckles rapping on her front door jolted her internal fantasies.

Instantly nervous, her breathing tight, she opened the door and found a man who wasn't at all Doug, nor a policeman – some tall friendly cowboy about her dad's age, looking down at her with a craggy smile as he removed his hat. "Dana Wilson?"

"Well – yes?"

He flapped a hefty police shield at her – like most people she didn't take time to look close at it. "I was just wondering if I might ask you a few questions about last night," he said in an almost kindly voice for a cop.

"You probably should talk to my husband."

"I'm sure you'll do fine."

The living room he walked into was identical in shape and size and building material to the one he'd been in up the path – but this living space was striking, immaculate, like a museum almost with exotic tapestries and crazy native artwork on the walls and tables, carved wooden statues of naked dancing aborigines and such placed here and there around the room. Complex Persian rugs adorned the otherwise nondescript wood floor, and there was a curious scent in the air – what was that?

"Please sit down," his hostess offered. Ty scanned the young lady visually, struck by her appearance. She was just a kid really, wearing the same sort of material on her body as was hanging on the walls, tapestry stuff but quite thin, almost see-through – looking very hip and snazzy for a seminary wife. These were curious times – girls running around with no bras, wearing dresses like hers that barely covered the essentials. Compared with his couple of years at Berkeley in the late thirties three decades ago, times were certainly on the move – but who could say why or where.

"So then," he said, shifting his mind to the police work at hand. He enjoyed questioning suspects and witnesses although down in Cambria, looking for who'd taken whose horses or cattle and so forth, it was a slightly different playing field. "You of course know what happened last night."

She was sitting balanced on a hand-crafted African stool just a few feet from him. "Yes," was all she said.

"I just got on the job this morning so I'm trying to catch up. Do you know when the shot was fired, did you hear it?"

"I did."

"You were in here at the time?"

"I was."

"At what time was the shot fired?"

"Around eleven I guess. I didn't look at a clock."

"You were here with your, uhm, husband?"

"He was gone."

"And his name please?"

"Stuart, Stuart Wilson."

"Ah yes. He was down at that meeting on some houseboat."

"Oh – you know about all that?"

"We end up learning about everything. That's our job. So you were alone."

"Yes."

"What were you doing, if I might ask – how focused were you on things like sounds?"

"Oh – I was, well … I was reading. There in that chair. A book by Camus. Have you read Camus?"

"A couple of his books. The Plague. The Stranger."

"Oh – a well-read cop?"

"Nights are long."

"You're not married?"

"Past tense. So last night did you hear anything else around that time?"

"Well – sure. There are half a dozen couples within a hundred feet here on this side of the hill, there's always sounds."

"Did you hear anything coming from the direction of the deceased's house – it's just next to you over there."

"Maybe I did. They weren't the quietest of couples."

"What was going on last night?"

"Their usual scene, him shouting. She was always quiet until he got rough. She'd shout at him if he hit her."

"Was last night a rough night?"

"I don't like gossiping about my neighbors."

"When one of those neighbors gets a bullet through his forehead, things change, wouldn't you say?"

"Is that what happened?"

"Bang – dead center."

"God. I can't believe it. I mean they fought, sure. But hey, Stu and I have our fights now and then, that's just normal, isn't it? But we don't shoot each other."

"Was she shouting back last night?"

"I told you – I'm not going to squeal."

"Okay then, off the record. Just help me get a sense of the reality of last night. It'll come out anyway, we're talking with all the neighbors."

"Oh. Well – so yeah, there was a sudden loud bout of shouting from over there, around twenty minutes or so before the sound of the gunshot. But ... it's so strange, don't you think? I mean, he was playing the pure innocent peace-loving Jesus all day and then when he was home like that, he'd revert to his old self. I thought he was cured, you know. That was the whole point."

"The whole point of what?"

"Jesus, Mister. You sure do push. What's your name anyway?"

"Ty."

"Well Ty," she said, re-crossing her legs and flashing more bare thigh than he'd seen in quite a while. "You said you don't know what's been happening here – you just landing from the moon or something?"

"I haven't been fully briefed on the details."

"Well it's no secret that Paul took a psychedelic and seemed to have been suddenly transformed. Into Jesus. I've known him for two years, ever since I met Stuart, they were friends back east. Everybody knew his nasty side when he drank but he'd never taken acid, his mom and his aunt were both schizoid, he was afraid he might flip and I'd say rightly so, based on what's happened. Now somebody goes in and kills him. Maybe serves him right – he was a wife-beater just as much as he was some mystic guru."

"You don't seem broken up by his death."

"Just because you know somebody doesn't mean you're close. Nobody was close to Paul if you want to know the truth. Not even Stuart. Paul was mostly lost in his head, actually not at all in to sex from what I could hear across the yard. Men in general, no offense meant, are imbeciles below the belt."

"Julia says she was leaving him."

"Well just between you and me, I'm the same – I've had it with Stu and this goddamn Seminary situation. This whole crazy trip's been one giant fiasco. And now what do we get? Murder. I tell you, I've had it."

"I hear you. So what about the meeting Stuart and Jon went to last night. I understand that two other Seminary students were at that meeting, uhm, Reggie – what's his last name again?"

"Davis. And probably ass-hole Doug."

"Yes, Douglas. I missed his last name too."

"McFerrin."

"You don't like him?"

"I almost called the cops on him last week."

"Why?"

"You sure do push."

"Sorry – just my job. So this meeting, I hear it was some kind of student revolutionary get-together."

"They take themselves so serious but really what can they do, what can anybody do? I'm as totally down on the war as the next person – napalming innocent women and children. We have no right at all to even be over there, murdering left and right with all our high technology. Still, I'm not the kind to riot out on the street."

"Tell me about Doug."

She made a face. "He's this older guy, some macho jet pilot who got shot down and came back from Nam with a limp. The guys worship him because after he got shot down and came back a hero, like overnight in some Army hospital he suddenly turned into a ranting anti-war protester. Doesn't mean anything, he's still a total creep – came over here one night last week when he knew Stuart was in Berkeley and I tell you, he was so slick I still don't believe it – had his fingers all over me and I do mean all over before I got to the point where I jabbed him in the eye."

She fell silent, bit out of breath with her face flushed. Ty cleared his throat, shifted his position, readjusted his Levi's. "So last night, let me get this straight. Paul and Julia had a verbal fight, maybe more. She left according to her account and went up to her friend Lucille – and then somebody came in and shot Paul. Is that what you think happened, or is there another version?"

She hesitated. She re-crossed her thighs. She looked Ty right in the eye. "They arrested Jon, right?"

"Yep."

"Well hold in mind, she was driving him crazy. If he did it then I say she made him do it. She was going over to his place all the time, behind Paul's back. Paul was gone usually down to the library, crazy about all the mystics this and mystics that of the church. You ask me, he was just finding an excuse to stay away from her, she liked getting laid and he didn't like laying her, you ask me.."

"So you and Julia aren't best of friends."

"She's pure bitch under all her oh-so-soft-and-lovey sex games. And then Jon went through a hard time when his wife left him. I tried to be nice to him, help him out — but Julia cut right in, acting like she was his best friend and all that but really just trying to get into his pants. And you bet she did — but now look what comes of it."

"Paul's death was a crime of passion?"

"What else could it be?"

"That's what we're trying to find out."

"I'll bet if Jon didn't do it, she did. Who else? And if he was the one who pulled the trigger, believe me, she provoked it."

9

In his stuffy sanitized cubicle at the San Anselmo station Jonathan was thinking related thoughts but coming to quite opposite conclusions – or rather coming to no conclusion – zilch. He'd just played half a dozen scenarios through his mind, but even his usually-brilliant synapses couldn't generate a satisfactory explanation of what had happened last night.

It was of course always possible that some crazy outsider religious nut had decided to kill Paul because he was acting and talking like he was the Christ and so he must be the anti-Christ. Or maybe some mean guy from Paul's seamy Brooklyn past finally caught up with him. Or it had been the CIA, who wouldn't flinch at murdering a radical in the sullied name of American peace and prosperity – look at what they'd done to Bobbie Kennedy not to mention his big brother and Martin Luther King and who knows who else.

But wait – how'd any of them known about the pistol being in that kitchen drawer? Only Julia had known where it was hidden and the fleeting thought that she'd shot Paul was ... an absolute no-go. The stunned look on her face when she'd run in and found the gun in Jon's hand was conclusive proof she hadn't shot Paul. So then – who did?

The omelet from some café down the street was good, Jonathan was surprised he had such an appetite. He wondered where he father was, what was happening on the outside? His dank tight solitary cell pressed in on him, he'd always had a thing about claustrophobia ever since getting stuck in a long dark culvert when he was four – but this wasn't the time for a claustrophobic freakout.

Alan came suddenly to mind, that comment that the CIA was after Tim Leary – was Paul's murder somehow related to Alan and Tim and the whole scene back at the Institute? That's where Jon had met Paul, after all. Paul had been hired as a hypnotic subject a few months after Jonathan had started working out there, but Paul lacked adequate susceptibility to the trance state so Bernie had moved the brilliant but moody New Yorker over to data analysis. But, why would the Institute want Paul dead – and why for that matter had Humphry's whole brain research project been so suddenly shut down, like Alan said?

Watch the breathing, put aside thoughts that stir up panic. Jon had learned loads of focusing games from Humphry and Bernie for stepping back and observing his breathing, his posture, his emotions and thoughts as they kept on erupting – but damnit, his pragmatic mind cut in and insisted, where was his dad, where was that lady cop, where was Alan? And closer to his heart just then, where was Julia? She'd need him right now, she was strong but almost too deep into her emotions – what would she be feeling right now?

Maybe he could tune into her – he'd gone through that complete set of transpersonal-projection experiments at the Institute, trying to document what the Russians already said they'd proven – that mutually-focused minds can communicate with each other from a distance ... so he gave it an internal-broadcast try. Julia, here I am. Focusing on you. Tuning into the air flowing in and out of my nose, expanding my awareness to fill my whole body, head to toe ... focusing on your presence here with me right now on this planet –

No, nothing. Humphry had been certain that focused compassion in the heart was what fueled transpersonal communication – hey Humphry, what's happening here, where are you, I need help, I need to plug back in with you, you were with my guide on my first LSD trip – please, come to me, help me!

... okay, nothing there – stop – I choose to quiet all those thoughts. Instead I'm now going to try another hypnosis condition we played with – I'm expanding another notch and filling the volume in this cell with my awareness ... now I'm expanding another step and filling this whole building – and now expanding way up and out to include Holy Hill. Hey please, Julia, are you there? Can you feel me? Julia?

Rather than directly contacting Julia, Jonathan suddenly found himself high up over trees and streets, looking down not exactly on Holy Hill but instead hovering in the crisp cool air over some big old house at the base of Holy Hill right next to the Presbyterian Church, several blocks from campus ... then unexpectedly and for no reason at all, that whole awareness bubble popped and left Jon sitting there utterly alone and muted.

In historic fact, right down inside that same house that Jonathan had ephemerally found himself hovering over, at that exact moment Reverend Wilma Blair's devoted housekeeper Stella was busy in the kitchen preparing coffee and nibbles while Wilma, senior pastor of the San Anselmo Presbyterian Church, pounded away at her typewriter writing an important press release. Stella had been with Wilma eight years now, their relationship was much more intimate than Wilma's congregation might imagine – and right now Stella was a nervous wreck because Wilma was in one of her funky moods.

The antique-chime doorbell rang. President Hurtz from the Seminary was at the door, a tall skinny man ten years Wilma's junior, an upstanding conservative gentleman. He nodded formally to Stella, whom he found far too young and pretty to be closeted away in a spinster's life. Stella led him silently into the large office/conference room.

"Ah Richard, there you are," Wilma intoned. Walking around the desk with her painful limp left over from an auto accident, she took his proffered hand in her bony arthritic grip. "Come and read what I've written thusfar."

More knocks on the door brought more members of the emergency committee-meeting into the room. First was Professor Rosenblum, that esteemed Old Testament master carrying his long walking staff but still quite agile at eighty-three. Arriving with him was a younger professor, a brilliant German-born woman named Ute Reinig, a tough loud-spoken theologian who'd suffered terribly through the War and now espoused a radical existential understanding of Christianity considered controversial in church circles but popular with her students.

Another member of the Committee knocked timidly a few moments later – psychologist Francis Cheek. Short, compact and always in a nervous rush, she was out of breath as she came into the relative darkness of the foyer. Almost on her heels came the student representative that the President had selected, Douglas McFerrin – a middle-aged former Air Force pilot of medium height with a noticeable limp but powerful torso (he did weights in his dorm room to keep in shape). As one of the few mature students, and in spite of his newly-espoused radical leanings, he had already helped as a student-administrative go-between during a couple recent controversies.

Doug entered the house fast, looking back behind him to make sure no one saw him go into this supposed bastion of conservative uptightness. He took off his leather jacket and gold-rimmed jet-pilot sunglasses he always wore, and walked stiffly but confidently into the study.

The others looked up at him from their chairs around the rectangular oak table. "Doug, glad you could make it," President Hurtz said. "Take a seat – coffee?"

There commenced a round of general mutterings about the murder before Richard called the meeting to order. "We have only half an hour," he pointed out, "before the community meeting up the hill. I'm sure you all know about Paul – such a terrible tragedy. And now one of our own students, Jon Hadley, is in jail for the heinous act. This horrendous event threatens to damage our seminary's reputation. We must make certain the outside world isn't fooled into thinking some bizarre Second Coming has taken place – we're gathered this morning to stave off such a misunderstanding."

"The campus is buzzing," Doug informed them, "students saying maybe the new Jesus actually appeared – and was murdered by a seminary student."

"Heretical!" Wilma blurted out, her fingers knitted in a tense knot. "And our service to the true Christ demands immediate action. Richard and I have prepared a press release – we seek your input before it goes out, although President Hurtz will make the final decision."

"Wilma," Richard said to her. "Perhaps you can read the document to the group."

She nodded, looked down through her bifocals at her typed page: "This weekend a personal tragedy has befallen two students at the San Francisco Theological Seminary. Jonathan Hadley has been arrested for fatally shooting fellow student Paul Jacobs. A preliminary police report indicates that Hadley used a pistol he brought illegally to the seminary. No other students were involved. Evidence indicates that Jacobs had taken an illegal psychotropic drug called LSD four days previously that caused a schizophrenic personality disorder, as diagnosed by resident psychologist Dr. Francis Cheek, that – "

"But wait, I didn't – "

"Hush Francis, please," the President said sternly. "Go on, Wilma."

"Taking this mind-altering drug apparently provoked an outbreak of multiple personality disorder in Jacobs, who at one point insisted that he had become Jesus Christ. This is a common psychotic condition, where mentally-ill individuals believe and act as if they are Napoleon, Jesus Christ, Julius Caesar and so forth."

"But Paul wasn't – "

"Francis, please!"

"Jacobs was approached by health professionals," Wilma continued with her reading, "but twice he refused psychiatric care. The San Anselmo Police say the shooting was almost certainly an act of passion. Hadley is being held without bail on first-degree murder. The Seminary deeply regrets this community tragedy, and will do everything possible to aid the authorities. President Richard Hurtz has declared Tuesday, February sixth as a

Seminary Day of Mourning; there will be no SFTS classes on that day."

Finished, Wilma looked up from the page. "Excellent, really," Douglas said. "That should do it. Send it off."

"Wait," Professor Reinig said in her German accent. "You are suggesting the Seminary forever judge young Paul as insane rather than inspired."

"Ute," Wilma retorted, "you're surely not suggesting that the Seminary accept any spiritual dimensions to Paul's mental instability."

"Jesus himself appeared out of obscurity speaking as if inspired by Spirit. Perhaps that historic event was also created by God coming into the mind of an average man."

"Heresy!" Wilma growled at her.

But the professor continued: "Tell me what proof you have that God was in fact not speaking through Paul, just as he spoke through his Son two thousand years ago."

"This is preposterous," Wilma accused her, eyes blazing with emotion. "If our seminary even for one moment appears to hint publically concerning that possibility, the entire religious world could explode."

"Wilma, there were reactionary religious authorities back in Jesus' day who felt exactly the same way you do."

"You speak hogwash, Professor. As a newcomer to our culture, you fail to understand how flammable the situation outside that door is right now – there's revolution stalking our land. Ask Douglas here."

Old Professor Rosenblum suddenly started coughing, his gaunt body caught in some emotional turmoil or health problem – breath raspy in his throat, lips pursed as if blocking something highly upsetting.

"You all right?" Doug asked.

"What? Of course – it is nothing – continue."

"Well Wilma is correct," Doug said. "Things are set to explode here on the west coast and back east too. If word gets spread that somebody shot down the new Jesus on a seminary campus, that could set off college violence."

"But what is our work as Christians all about," Ute insisted, "if not to help pave the way for the Second Coming. I was very moved by Paul. I had not yet determined exactly how genuine his inner source of spiritual insight was – but I challenge Dr. Cheek to produce legal evidence verifying that Paul was in any way mentally insane."

"It's true, I agree, there is no evidence," the therapist insisted. "And it would be entirely un-Christian to do such a heinous thing to that dead man's reputation."

Professor Rosenblum banged his ancient fist against the table. "You idiots," he shouted. "Paul was actively destroying Christian beliefs that are sacred! He was agr– "

A fit of coughing and choking, silenced the professor. Tears ran down his face as his emaciated frame shook with some internal tremor of emotion or illness.

"Should we call a doctor?" Wilma offered.

"No – no," the old man managed to mutter. "I am simply outraged, outraged that any Christian would sit here and defend that man's heresy of claiming to be our Savior. We must act immediately to silence the despicable rumors."

Miss Streep re-entered the room. "Excuse me but there are two men in the foyer."

"Ah, finally," Richard said. "Bring them in."

A rather podgy fifty-year-old man who looked like an efficient mid-range executive entered the room, followed by a tall tight-lipped man of about thirty-five, also in coat and tie but wearing black-rimmed sunglasses. As he condescended to remove them, he glanced quickly with high-alert eyes at each person in the meeting, then returned to Douglas whom he stared at blankly – then looked away.

President Hurtz was walking around the table to shake hands. "For those of you who don't already know him," he intoned with high respect, "let me introduce the head of our Presbyterian General Assembly, Dr. Logan Millway from New York. And this other gentleman is from the Central Intelligence Agency, Thomas Quill."

As Miss Streep brought two more chairs, Richard introduced the members of the committee. "I recommend, as time is of the essence," Wilma spoke up, "that you read the press release we're sending out – this is urgent business."

She handed them each a copy and everyone waited silently as they read the short document. "Yes," Dr. Logan concluded, quite pleased. "The wording is impeccable."

Wilma nodded with her jutting chin, then looked across to the CIA man. "I've done my best to keep abreast of recent terrorist activities among our young – Weathermen, Black Panthers and so forth. Sir – please advise us."

"Well no question, the situation on the streets has become extreme, all the kids lack is a charismatic leader or martyr. I just reviewed TV footage of the deceased talking at your local church here. Jacobs was definitely a leader with a radical message and he could have provoked serious trouble. That danger has been averted – but we still face this rather moribund possibility of people crying out that the new Jesus has been killed. This press release, stating the incidence of mental illness, should help dispel that danger. I advise that you send it out immediately. And do everything possible on campus to quell further discussion."

"But I once again must speak," the German professor said directly to the government agent. "I ask you as one Christian to another, if I might make that assumption – theologically do you hear what it is that you're saying?"

"I'm concerned about the internal safety of our nation, Ma'am. The Communist influence on campuses and the slums is on red-alert. We must squash it."

"You are speaking from fear, not from a loving Christian state – just as the authorities reacted in fear when they killed the historic Jesus."

"Hey, this is Reality 101 I'm talking here, not some Existential Bible Study. And Paul Jacobs was most assuredly not anywhere near Christ status – just the opposite. Back at NYU he was a player in both SDS and the Weathermen."

"Yes, Paul openly told us all that in class," she countered. "He said he had done nothing illegal, he came here to seminary to seek a more peaceful path."

"That man was an inveterate liar, a borderline schizophrenic sporting several personalities."

"Do you have even a single shred of evidence to prove your point?" Ute demanded.

"Suffice it to say that Mister Jacobs was under serious government observation."

"Wait – are you saying," Francis Cheek blurted out, "that you actually have spies on our campus?"

"We do what we legally can to thwart anti-American activities. Do you want Weatherman terrorist groups next door, Black Panthers bombing your grammar school, poisoning your water?"

"I know from personal experience, working last summer in Oakland," Dr. Cheek insisted, "that many Black Panthers are noble young men and women struggling to help their communities rise up from crime and poverty. We even have a former Black Panther here on campus, Reggie Davis."

"As we well know," Agent Thomas said calmly.

"Well Reggie said the same as Paul," Ute claimed. "He's seeking a more spiritual path."

"That's just another of the clever lines of Communist sympathizers out to scalp your children's souls."

"So then," Ute grumbled at him, "You don't want people becoming excited about Jesus having perhaps come to us through Paul – so you decide to squash an innocent young man's reputation. I for one will not allow it!"

"I must inform you," President Hurtz told her hotly, "that if you cause problems with this, you risk losing your position at this seminary."

"You wouldn't dare!"

"I mean really, Ute," Wilma interjected, "just because you had some kind of crush on a psychotic – grow up."

"Enough!" The President of the seminary stood up. "I thank you all for coming on such short notice. We must act immediately to catch the press deadline. May

God be with us all – see you up at the community meeting."

Everyone got up silently and started for the door. As Ute passed Wilma, she paused. "Congratulations," the German woman said bitingly, "you've quite efficiently crucified that young man, whoever he was. So much for Christian fairness and compassion."

10

Ty came walking fast up Holy Hill from the cottages to the top parking lot. Kate was sitting in her car taking notes on a big yellow pad. He got in the passenger side and closed the door against the slight chill in the breeze. Inside it was warmer – he wondered if it was her body heat that had warmed the interior, there was a slight musty scent in the air that he liked.

She kept working with diligence on her notes for a moment without looking at him. He unbuttoned his Levi jacket a few notches, settled his long body into the seat. She snapped her notebook shut.

"So," she said. "Thanks for doing Stuart and Dana, I can go again if you found anything."

"Just a bit," he drawled.

"You're a strange one," she told him.

"I assume that's a compliment."

Their eyes locked a moment, as they had several times previously that morning. Both of their expressions were sober – but then she gave him a fleeting soft smile. "Okay, then. What did they have to say, get out your notes."

"I don't take notes. Stuart wasn't home. Dana, she's a sexy one – just a kid really. Did her best at first not to answer with anything more than a yes or a no, then started blabbing and couldn't stop."

"You like young girls."

"Nice to look at. Big bother otherwise. But she heard Paul and Julia arguing last night twenty minutes before he was shot. A recurrent event if you believe Dana Stuart."

"Anything else?"

"Douglas McFerrin, an older student who was at that houseboat meeting, he supposedly tried to force himself on Dana. Reginald Davis, a friend of Stuart's and Doug's, was another houseboat attendee. They seem to be caught up in anti-war stuff. Dana claims to be splitting up with her husband. I think she was hot for Jon herself and jealous of Julia for winning so she's throwing suspicion at Julia. If Paul was beating up his wife, who knows? And Dana herself was there alone next door — she could have pulled the trigger."

He fell quiet. She kept her eyes on him. "So — you're good," she acknowledged.

"You ask people enough questions the right way, the truth usually comes out."

"For a cowboy you seem to know proper procedure."

"Once a year they send me off for training during the winter when things slow down on the ranch."

"Well good — this isn't going to be easy. Lucille Gearhart in the cottage Julia ran to last night, she also says Paul abused Julia when he drank. Last night around ten-thirty Julia came up crying because of Paul but refused to call the police. Strange, don't you think, somebody going around being Jesus by day, turning into a wife-hitter by night."

"Maybe Paul had a schizoid edge to him," Ty guessed. "I had a wife who was mostly sweet but suddenly violent."

"Oh?"

"Suicide finally – hit Jonathan even harder than me."

"How long ago?"

"Maybe ten years. And in comparison I'd say that for Paul, the LSD thing pushed his condition. Who knows what he might have ended up doing if he hadn't been shot. Hey, let's head down the hill, I need to talk to Jonathan."

She nodded, started up the cruiser and drove off down the hill at an even pace. "You're locked right in on this, aren't you."

"You mind?"

"As long as you go for the truth rather than what you want for your boy."

"I told him on the phone I can't help him if he's guilty. My dad put his own brother in jail for rustling horses."

"Your dad in law enforcement?"

"Part-time deputy sheriff. I took over his job when he got killed. What about you – where's that accent from?"

She eyed him. "You're so smart, you guess."

"Somewhere north of here, east a bit. Washington? I go cattle-buying every Fall up there. You a Spokane girl?"

"East about a hundred miles, just out of McCall."

"Ah, I buy from the Bulhursts over in Long Valley. I don't recall running into the Douglas clan."

"Dad doesn't sell off his calves, they winter at a feedlot he owns out of Caldwell."

"So – a country girl."

"Used to be."

"What happened, did some handsome city guy come up and grab you?"

She shrugged her shoulders. "I came down to Berkeley – long song."

"Sing it for me sometime. Right now, you gotta understand, I want Jonathan."

The stuffy room was small with off-white walls and a heater fan, typical low-end interrogation situation. Ty walked in and found his son sitting there slouched like some common criminal – it made him feel terrible inside but he blocked its expression.

"Dad."

"Jonnie. You look like hell, son."

"Well you not much better."

"At least I'm breathing good clean air out there. Redwoods got their own country presence. Hey, the new Amazing Rhythm Aces album's out, you heard it yet?"

Without further ado, Ty produced a small battery-run tape player he sometimes took with him in the Jeep, put it on the table between them, pushed a button and a song started up sporting a hot fast steel guitar lead with a brilliant edge of slinky-jazz phrasing.

"I think they got Buddy Emmons in for those studio licks," Ty said, nodding to the tape player.

A raspy male singer's voice, the essence of cowboy, took over the song. The machine's tonal quality was tinny but the sound filled the room, just as Ty expected. "Situations like this, always assume there's people listening in," he said quietly, leaning forward with his elbows on the table. "Best to muffle whatever it is you tell me. This is entirely out of hand, you being here stuck in this goddamn jail."

They looked square into each other's eyes. The kid was doing his best to stay tough. Ty reached over and put his sun-tanned work-calloused hand temporarily on his son's forearm in a gesture that made Jon feel suddenly about a thousand times better.

"I already been checking things," Ty told him. "Quite a little bee hive. At least we got a cop with horse sense. So tell me what happened."

Jonathan's version of the night before wasn't much different than what Ty had already heard. He leaned back. "Okay then," he said, "where exactly were you when you heard that shot?"

"Fifty feet up the path from Paul's house."

"Headed there or to your place?"

"I wasn't sure – just coming home."

"Where'd you been?"

"Meeting."

"What kind of meeting?"

"You know, just guys getting together."

"You and who else?"

"Uhm – Doug McFerrin, older guy with a limp. Stuart. Reggie. Few others."

"I want full names – spit it."

"Dad, don't treat me like you're a fuckin' cop."

Ty eyed him hard. Sighed his trademark exhale – pushed himself back from the table and stood up to leave.

"Hey," from Jon.

"If you don't want to cooperate, I'm right now out'a here. We've got a dozen calves need penicillin, hundred yards of fence down, pump needs to go into town, gotta finish disking the barley field, not to mention a goddamn fermentation disaster with the grapes – Chris is way over his head trying to run the place until I get back."

"What about cousin Benjy, I thought he was helping you these days."

"Bah – Ben's down in Cambria with some boobsie girlfriend writing a new spy novel. He's been no good for nothing since he went off to college and then it was you, got him working out at that goddamn Institute. Fucked up both your minds. And your other renegade cousin, he got a phone call last week and took off for Afghanistan or some place – we'd had a bit of a row a couple of weeks ago. So it's hard times at the place and you hear me clear – I don't have no time at all to fart around up here."

"Sorry. Uhm. I'm just totally fried in the nerves, Dad, no sleep at all last night. Please, really – help me."

"Well it's like this – you tell me one falsehood and I'm out that door. I've got to crack this thing open fast."

"Yeah. Gotcha. Crack away."

Ty relaxed a notch, got himself comfortable again on his chair. A new song started up, fast blue-grass picking with Dobro interlacing – tasty. "Tell me about the meeting, what's with this Watts guy?"

"Dad, it's all real complex. You're never going to understand the situation – you're living out in nowhere, you've got no idea what's happening in the world."

"You'd be surprised."

"Well yeah, you're probably the only guy in the whole valley who reads the New Yorker. Sometimes I think you'd have been happier in our life working as a real city cop."

"That was your mom, she got me reading the New Yorker. So come on, what about that houseboat scene? Katie – she's our cop here – she says this Mister Watts is the head of some radical suspect fringe group."

"Fuck that. Alan's a spiritual genius teaching us how to live more harmoniously – basic early Christian stuff that the church totally lost touch with. Alan started out as an Episcopal minister, Mom would have liked him. And he just wanted to help Paul. That's what the meeting at his houseboat was all about."

"Well – this guy Paul didn't get much help last night, did he. And I hear it was you who pushed him to take LSD."

"Wrong entirely – Stuart did the pushing. I told Paul ten times he shouldn't drop acid. You know I worked at the LSD research center back east and – "

"Major mistake there."

" – and I got trained professionally, federally licensed and all the rest, to guide subjects in experiments so yeah, I did what I could to keep Paul's trip positive. I guess maybe I did a little too good a job. I'd explained to Paul he should take mushrooms, psilocybin, not LSD – mushrooms are organic and they last just a few hours compared to ten to twelve with acid."

"My son, the world's expert on narcotics."

"LSD's not a narcotic. And yeah, I am an expert, the Institute was the leader in psychedelic research, all federally funded. I told you the whole ting this summer, I was trained as a research facilitator. I ended up guiding most of the Berkeley math and physics profs this summer vacation, after you told me I couldn't hang out at the ranch."

"That was my fraternal responsibility with a son taking drugs and talking about being on the run from the CIA – you were over the edge and you wouldn't listen to reason. Then off you went into this whole seminary situation – I knew all along you were doing this minister gambit to dodge the draft."

"Well forgive me," Jon said belligerently, "if I refuse to go kill innocent women and children in Vietnam. Besides, Mom brought me up Presbyterian so yeah, here I am at their seminary. I've been doing my best to fit in here, dead serious, looking to find some light in Mom's religious tradition – but hey, it's fucking hard, there's been just too much non-stop fear-based manipulatory brain-washing and all the religious wars and politics and all the rest of the perennial priestly-cult bullshit as Alan calls it."

"Enough – time's real tight just now, there's a Seminary meeting up the hill I need to go catch. By the way, somebody rampaged your place early this morning looking for something. What exactly were they looking for, tell me now."

Jonathan made a face. "Nothing to find there."

Father and son stared each other down but Jon remained stubbornly mum. "Alright, we'll come back to that," Ty grumbled. "So now quick, tell me your opinion on the whole 'Paul into Jesus' thing."

"Hmm Well. That's almost impossible to talk about. I mean it was totally real and right and real and at the same time, just absolutely crazy. I admit I led him in that general direction, helped him focus on having a positive spiritual experience, I read to him from some of his Gnostic texts – but I was never fully in charge of his experience. LSD's an atomic bomb compared to local fireworks, it packs the chemical power even in a tiny amount, a hundred micrograms, to totally awaken the brain. What it does according to Humphry is temporarily turn off the whole sensation-filtering mechanism of the diencephalon so that the whole brain fires off at once – it's an amazing mental tool and you're definitely never the same after taking it, that's why it's called a trip – you experience a million new experiences in ten hours, it's similar to how I was never the same after I came back from that exchange year in South Africa."

"Well that was different – you came home to deal with your mom being dead."

"Yeah – anyway. But I admit, I feel at least partly responsible for Paul's shift into Jesus. I did my absolute best but Paul was a strange guy from the start, packing an amazing mind and destined for something great if only he could learn to handle his emotions, his rages. That was our main intent – but even with my help, look at what happened."

"Bullet in the head – you tell me who did it."

"I've wracked my brains. I just don't know."

"What about Dana. I talked to her, saw more female skin than I asked for. You think she shot Paul?"

"Anything's possible but what's her motive?"

"Jealousy maybe," Ty guessed. "And just to cover all bases, what about Julia as the shooter?"

"I told you she came in after me, not before me."

"She could have gone in, shot him, gone out the back door and then come in again after you."

"She'd never kill Paul and frame me."

"She in love with you?"

Jonathan frowned. "Maybe. But that doesn't matter – she didn't do it."

"So who did?"

"Hey, there were dozens of nasty right-wing weirdoes shouting Paul down during his talks, and also there were some threatening phone calls. Could have been some nutcase out to kill the AntiChrist, walked into the cottage and saw the gun – bang."

Ty was silent. The music was cooking away nice and loud on the tinny player. He glanced at his watch –

the campus meeting was in twenty minutes. "You talked to Paul earlier that evening. Was there conflict between you and him?"

"Hardly. We knew how to get along, ever since he came to the Institute from NYU, got the job working with us. When he wasn't drinking he was a real deep beautiful guy. He lived way inside himself, everybody wanted to get close to Paul but nobody did, not even Julia."

"She told me about you and her."

"Oh. Well that just happened. She was lonely. And I was alone. Paul just didn't need her. He didn't need anybody."

"They're calling the murder a crime of passion. If you in fact did shoot him then that's the best story to hold on to."

"Goddamn – I didn't kill him!"

"The pistol you say you gave Julie, tell me why you did that."

"Because of the threatening phone calls. Well, and also for the last few nights, Paul got real strange – their relationship was on the rocks anyway, she'd already told him she was leaving him but he was in the ozone off somewhere, he just didn't seem to want to process the information."

"You saying he was crazy?"

"Not exactly but recently, he'd got overly caught up reading the early Gnostic notions of some mystic Second Coming, and then there came that New Yorker article documenting psilocybin mushrooms being used by the early Gnostic mystics – but was he crazy? Was Jesus crazy? They did eat magic mushrooms in ceremony over in Lebanon, you know, way back then."

"Yeah, I read that article."

"So Paul got more and more manic, reading all those ancient manuscripts ten hours a day. I started to think in fact that a trip might help him, Humphry had guided me on my first trip and it worked just great – but that's not the point here, Dad. The fucking real danger is that there's still somebody out there who did murder Paul in cold blood, and that means that Julia's maybe also in danger – and I'm fuckin' stuck here behind bars where I can't do a goddamn thing. Please, you stick real close to her tonight. Promise me."

"So you're serious in love this time."

Their eyes met. "Looks like it."

"Well you could do worse, she's a good person. Real good." He looked at his watch again and stood up. "I gotta go monitor that community meeting up the hill. You might have to sit here a day or two, be patient. Anything else, quick?"

"Richard Hurtz who runs the Seminary, he tried yesterday to get Julia to put Paul away as a nut-case but we said absolutely not – I mean, you should have heard the things Paul was saying, he really might have been Jesus, Dad – he was that right on. Not acting, not crazy – he could see something beyond us, he saw what makes humans tick and what we might do to tick better, you know?"

"No, not really – but we'll talk later." Ty turned off the tape player. "Keep the machine," he said. "Play it during interviews, be real careful what you say right now to anybody."

"Another key thing – a friend of mine filmed the last three talks Paul gave. Guy's name is Rupert Maddox. Student at the seminary. Look him up quick and keep those flicks safe, they're all that remains of Paul. Maybe there's some clue there. Rupert lives in the singles dorm. And dammit, be careful – there's a killer out there."

"Yeah. I'm staying in your cottage. Julia can take your bedroom, me the couch. Gotta run – and rest easy, you know me, we'll nab whoever shot your buddy."

Ty knocked on the door. It opened and Kate stood there. "Someone else to see you," she told Jon.

Outside in the hallway there was a man around thirty-five or forty with big muscles bulging under his shirt. He walked past Ty and into the interview room, wearing dark glasses in the dark, and sporting a limp.

Kate closed the door and Ty suddenly found himself alone in a temporarily-deserted dim-lit hallway with this women cop who had somehow already got under his skin in a way he suspected he liked. Now she was standing close to him but not saying anything, not doing anything – just looking up at him with those penetrating eyes of hers, generating a feeling inside him like they already had something serious going.

"Uhm," he managed to say, his voice a bit gruff, "is that guy's name Douglas McFerrin?"

She was silent a moment, then said very quietly. "You must have antennas."

"Just the one."

"You're not talking dirty to me, are you?"

"Not yet. You enjoy the Amazing Rhythm Aces?"

"I have that album myself, bought it last week."

"Do you have tape running on them right now?"

She didn't answer him. Ty became acutely aware of her breathing sounds, and that slight half-perfume, half-organic smell of her. "Uhm, what did you just say?" she finally asked in a very quiet voice.

"Are you taping them?"

"What do you think?"

This time on his side, one, two breaths went by. "I think that being alone like this with you in this dark police alley makes me feel, uhm, unusual."

Rather than respond verbally to his words, she exhaled loud through the mouth, reached without warning and grabbed a handful of his shirt, and pushed him back against the wall.

"Damn you, this isn't what your son in there needs," she grumbled at him, and then walked off down the hallway.

Jonathan didn't get up as Doug came limping with his usual cocky demeanor into the room and sat down across the metal table from him. Jon was surprised and not entirely pleased at the new visitor. Doug was Stuart's friend but Doug and Jon had never quite warmed to each other during the four months they'd been students together at the seminary. Doug carried his ex-Air Force attitude like a proud superior badge and Jon didn't really enjoy the attitude.

"So," Doug began, leaning back in the chair. "This is totally crazy, isn't it. Paul dead and you in here."

"Yep."

"So I just came to see how you're doing and if there's anything I can do to help."

"Yeah – go find out who shot Paul and hand him over to the police."

"We're all pushing for that, you can trust us."

"So then tell me," Jon asked, "who's top on your hit list?"

"Nobody would shoot Paul."

"Somebody did."

"Maybe some toughs from back East? Anyway I just wanted to touch base, let you know you're not alone. Who was that visiting you, the cowpoke?"

"That's my father. And if anybody can solve this, he can."

"John Wayne type, hey?"

"What do you want, Doug? Out with it."

"Oh, you know, I was just wondering – say, is that a tape player, can we play something?"

"I suppose."

Doug pushed and the Amazing Rhythm Aces sang another tune. "Ah, better," from Doug. "Anyway, I was just wondering if I can help you out with the stuff, you know, move it to a better place, more secure."

"It's entirely secure. No more talk."

"Things are heating up, we're off to Oakland this afternoon for some meetings regarding what we were talking about. Maybe before you're out of here we need to act. I can help that along if you tell me the locale."

"No – get outa here."

"You can trust me, Jon. Honest to God."

"Which God, the one that had you over in Nam napalming women and children?"

"I've made my peace with what I did, I was like all the rest, I had to get nearly killed to wake up but I'm awake now, Jon. Please. We'll cut you in on profits but mostly it's for the cause, blow some mass minds, wake people up – that's our only hope."

Jon eyed him a moment. "No. No. No."

"Just like that?"

"Just like that."

Jon reached, turned off the music – stood up and went over to the door and banged on it.

"But you might be in here for years, the evidence against you is rock solid," Doug told him with a harder edge to his voice. "This might be your last time to hand over the power to the people."

Jon turned and faced him. "I said no."

11

Rupert with his camera got there just in time, the whole auditorium was full, people talking loud, half of them still standing rather than taking seats on the folding chairs. Up front President Hurtz was on the stage talking with the pastor from the local church who as usual was dressed in a dark pants suit that made her look more male than female since she hardly had any breasts to speak of.

All eyes were looking forward to the front of the hall while Rupert quickly set up his tripod, then got his dad's old 16 mm camera in place and screwed it down tight. Coming from a Hollywood documentary family, he knew this footage would be an important part of his larger cinematic concept so he worked fast to get the focus tight so that –

Two pairs of strong hands grabbed him from behind, lifted his slim frame into the air and carried him backward, right on out of the auditorium. He was so shocked, and the hands so painfully in control, that he failed to shout in resistance before his mouth was covered with a strong male hand. Two men in suits commenced to half-drag him away from the meeting, back down toward the dorms.

Ty and Kate had taken seats and, like everybody else, were busy watching the President approaching the lectern, not looking to the back of the auditorium when

Rupert entered, a bit late, and started setting up. However, Ty by pure chance happened to glance around him at the audience and the movement in back of the room caught the edge of his eye. He turned and looked just as the cameraman disappeared through the back doors, leaving the camera standing there all alone.

No one else seemed to notice what had happened, but Ty's gut muscles tensed. "I'm back in ten, you stay here," he told Kate, and worked his way fast along the side aisle to the back door where he'd seen two men absconding with a third. As he came busting outside he spied the threesome as they disappeared down a back path. He took off running after them, rounding a corner just in time to see them take the kid in through the front door of the singles dormitory.

The door closed as Ty approached. He waited for two breaths, then cautiously opened it and entered the building. This was his first possible lead in the case and he didn't want to blow it. As he moved through the relative darkness, listening to the scuffing of feet going up the interior stairs, he suddenly wished he'd brought Kate with him.

Reaching inside his Levi jacket, he brought out the .38 as a reflex move. Kidnapping of some sort had just taken place so he had a right to bear arms. The two aggressors seemed to be wearing the kind of suits and ties that Mormons went around in – or that the FBI was fond of. Didn't matter to Ty, a lead was a lead and his son's freedom was at stake.

He knew how to move quiet and fast in cowboy boots – and as he looked around the corner at the top of the stairs he was just in time to catch movement as bodies disappeared through the fourth doorway down to the left. He got to the door but found it locked. He could vaguely hear a low menacing voice and then a mumbled defiant reply and then the sound of the kid getting slapped hard and crying out in pain.

With no thought of consequences Ty took a step back and whammed his shoulder against the door. It splintered on the first heave, then gave entirely as the door jam came loose with the second. But they were on him so fast he didn't see it coming – wham! Down he went crashing in a sudden slump to the floor with the wind knocked out of his solar plexus.

The kid definitely had gumption, grabbing something and clobbering one of the two guys right over the head. The second guy instantly swung his leg with a practiced karate move and flattened the kid – then grabbed his buddy and dragged him from the room, skedaddling down the hallway before Ty could manage to sit upright, let alone go chasing after them.

And so they sat in aftermath, the kid nursing all sorts of temporary but highly painful indignities including a luckily-slight swelling down in the left testicle. The older guy had fared better, quickly recovering from the one solid sock to the chest. He fumbled around on the messy floor and found his pistol.

"Fuck!" the kid managed to mutter.

"Double that," Ty agreed. "So who were they, what was that all about?"

"Mmmhh," from Rupert as he managed to come onto hands and knees.

Catching his breath, Ty stood up and looked around the room. "Tell me, what were they after?"

"Mmph."

"Was that related to you filming Paul yesterday?"

Rupert managed to move back into a sitting position on the floor, then stared blankly at the grown cowboy in his room. "Who – who are you anyway?"

"Fifth cavalry. That'll cost you a dollar. I'm Ty Hadley – Jonathan is my boy. I just talked to him at the jail and he told me to come see you and take care of the film you shot of Paul."

"You – Jonathan's dad?"

"Yep."

"You've gotta help him – he didn't do it."

"So who did?"

"How about those two turds?"

"Do you know who they were?"

"Never saw them before."

"I hope you don't ever again. Heavy players and definitely not Mormons."

"They were after my film – they want to destroy the evidence, get rid of Paul entirely. I knew I should have sent it all off earlier."

"Off where?"

"To my dad to process. The world has a right to see Paul being Jesus. Something important, gigantic, happened here and I caught some of it on film, my dad will be proud. But wait – did you say Jon told you about me, about the documentary?"

"Half an hour ago – he said the films you have should be protected and preserved. But no, I didn't talk to anybody about you, those guys already knew."

"Well yeah, I was out in plain sight – nobody ever thought for even a minute that Paul, you know, that somebody …"

"You've no idea who shot him?"

"When we watch the footage, you know, we might see something."

"My thought exactly. So listen – can I take your films to the local police and let them do the processing? They're going to be evidence in the murder anyway, you'll have to hand them over. I'll guarantee you get the originals back."

"Right now I'm just afraid – and I don't even really know you are who you say you are."

Ty showed him his shield.

"Okay then," Rupert said. "Yes, take them."

"And maybe you shouldn't hang around this place for the next few days – you have friends somewhere you can go until I give you a call?"

"I guess my uncle."

"He close to your dad?"

"They hardly talk. Uncle Tom is a capitalist pig, Dad's a flaming liberal. I manage to get along with both, they're sort of all I've got."

"Sounds okay – here's the plan."

Julia woke up in her own bed, disoriented from her nap. Slowly regaining her senses, she remembered taking a long vague bath, and then lying down. Now, rising up from sleep, she was able to enjoy just a few blank moments of relative peace before she got hit with the gross remembrance – Paul was dead, Jon in jail – and her own shaken life very much in the ozone. Perhaps she should call her mother.

She sat up and ran her fingers through her tousled head of hair. Her eyes looked out the side window at Jon's cottage and a memory came to her from back when she'd first moved in here – glancing out this same window across the fifty feet of redwood trunks and vaguely seeing two naked people having sex together in Jonathan's bedroom.

Somehow, she thought to herself now, it had been sexual from the start – he'd attracted her from a distance that kept becoming less distant until she herself was the one in bed with him. She hadn't known him back east but he'd known Paul well, it seemed. And it had all happened so naturally. A couple of weeks after Jon's wife had left him and gone back home, Julia had gone over casually to talk with Jon one afternoon while Paul was as usual down at the library. Jon had been such a good listener that she'd found herself unexpectedly breaking down, confessing to him how lonely and sometimes even afraid she was, living with Paul.

Before either of them knew it they were holding hands, the conversation dropping away. And then, ten days later, with Jon finally fully inside her, he'd awoken her to feelings she'd never experienced with Paul – an urgent but still gentle softness to his hardness, a much slower lover's pace, and especially some new quality of heart contact and genuine, innocent tenderness.

She turned away from the window. Had all that been wrong? In breaking her marriage vows had she violated something sacred? No, she assured herself, just the opposite – she'd discovered feelings that were genuinely sacred with Jon and entirely missing with Paul. And now, fearing that absolutely everything was lost, she sat on the bed just trying to get a grip, wondering what on earth she should do?

Suddenly someone was rapping loudly on her front door. "Hello, hello … anyone home?"

She recognized that deep gravelly voice – it was old Professor Rosenblum. She'd gone with Paul and another couple to dinner at the fellow's home a few weeks ago before Paul had turned into Jesus and somehow angered the old man. Hesitantly, emerging from the bedroom, she went and opened the front door.

The stooped figure stood there before her, holding his long wooden walking staff that he always carried even though he was still quite agile. But today his ancient expression was gaunt, almost frightening to behold. "Ah, so you are still here," he said. She noticed he was wearing an old-fashioned gentleman's fedora hat on his head.

"Well – yes, I'm here. Please, come in."

"I have only a moment," he said gruffly in his terse European accent, walking into the relative darkness of the cottage, "I'm driving myself today, Norrie's at the dentist. How are you holding together? People you love dying violent deaths – I have known too much of that myself. I've come to see, well, to see if you need help."

She felt suddenly touched by his overt show of compassion, considering how angry he'd been about Paul's shift into Jesus mode. She took his arm to guide him to the sofa but he stopped walking and stared at Paul's easy chair.

"So is that where you found him?" he asked.

"Oh – yes."

"Shot in the head."

"Yes."

"Removed from any further action in this world."

"Do sit down," she said, and led him to the sofa. "Would you like some tea?"

"No, no. You see, Norrie is concerned that you are in this house where the murder took place, she said she can come and stay with you, or you come stay with us. Also we want to invite you for dinner tonight."

"That's very kind of you."

"But right now you and I, we must talk. This is all so impossible, there has recently been a haze before my eyes, why must the good life always degenerate into hellish times! False prophets shall always arise but ... well – just moments ago I could see all this almost clearly, but now – I am here to tell you, we must – "

Someone started knocking at the front door and then a quiet male voice spoke from outside. "Julie, it's me, Ty."

"Ah, good – that's Jonathan's father," she said, and went with relief to open the door. The old man seemed half crazed and she was acutely uncomfortable being alone with him.

Ty walked in, removed his hat and noticed the old man in the room. "Oh, I don't mean to disturb," he said.

Looking upset by the intrusion, the Professor stood up. "I was just leaving," he grumbled.

"Professor, this is Ty Hadley, Jon's father. Ty, this is Professor Rosenblum, he teaches Old Testament at the seminary."

Ty shook the proffered claw. "Wait – are you the professor that Rupert shot some movies of?"

"Rupert, yes. Movies. The crazy boy with the camera, filming me as the prophets emerged one after the other. Yes, I am the one – but then Paul, he ruined everything, he just had to go and – but no, enough. I must get home. I only came to talk to – to invite Julia to dinner tonight."

"Well why don't you come over to Jonathan's house tonight," Ty offered. "Julia and I have it all planned already, and the detective handling the murder will be dining with us. If you knew Paul, perhaps you can offer some insights."

"I – well indeed. Indeed yes. Insights. You must understand, this tragedy is entirely different than meets the eye. Your son did not kill Paul, of that I can assure you."

"Do you have evidence we can use?"

The old man looked blankly at Ty a long moment, as if losing his thread of thought – then turned his head and looked at Paul's empty easy-chair. "Evidence – not exactly. But I know here in my heart, truth must out. God is the victor. No one stands high enough to block God's light. But I must go. What time tonight, six? Red wine or white? And would you like Norrie to bring a salad – she'll insist on bringing something."

"Well yes," Julia said, "a salad will be helpful."

"Good, good. Tonight is the proper time, I shall speak to the police officer. This is now settled."

"But please," Ty pushed, "tell me what you know now, not later. This investigation can't wait till tonight."

"Do not push me, young man!"

"Well. Alright then – tonight. At six. Next door."

The professor turned and started walking out of the living room. Julia moved forward to help him but he pushed her away. "I am not an invalid," he grumbled.

He closed the door with a slight slam behind him. "Grumpy old guy," Ty said, standing alone with Julia. "What do you think he knows – what was the story between him and Paul?"

"Paul was his best student, asking deep questions about the prophets, about the inner connection there must have been between them and God. I went to the Professor's lectures too, he had this amazing ability to go into character and act out the biblical speeches of Old Testament prophets, it was like going to the theater. But in class last Wednesday Paul started suddenly doing the same – but speaking with the authority of Jesus himself, and the Professor became instantly upset – aghast that Paul dared to talk with such power."

"Do you think the old man knows something that could free Jon?"

She thought a moment. "No, I doubt it. He only comes down to campus to give his lectures, otherwise he's up at his home in retreat. I think he just feels certain in his heart, like he said, that Jon could never kill anybody."

She noticed the rumpled brown paper bag that Ty was holding. "What's that, something for dinner?"

"Uhm, no. Listen, I'm starting to fade, I need to grab a nap. Let's go on over to Jon's and settle in."

12

Stuart owned a fine old black '37 Packard sedan, its long sleek lines looking as if royalty was driving through San Anselmo instead of a triage of local seminary students. Nobody around campus knew quite what to make of Stuart – he was 27 and obviously very smart, he was usually friendly but always seeming to be playing a dozen half-hidden games at once behind your back. He'd started college at NYU, been drafted early and sent to Nam – then he'd spent a few years traveling the world seeking spiritual teachers and so forth before returning to finish at NYU. So in contrast to his small circle of seminary buddies, he obviously wasn't avoiding the draft by attending seminary; furthermore, having grown up in the shadow of a highly-successful father (whom he considered a capitalistic pig deserving the very worst) he knew how money was made, so that wasn't his driving life issue.

Stuart by his own admittance was officially encamped at the San Francisco Theological Seminary to unearth hidden esoteric dimensions of his religious heritage. But quite privately he was also using the seminary as a perfect base of operations for covert participation in radical organizations such as the Students for a Democratic Society, which he'd joined originally back at NYU. Even though to his seminary professors he was one of their most promising budding theologians, to his close friends he was more like a quiet fanatic waging his secret war against all Americans making money by waging war in Vietnam – this was once his holy cause. But after ingesting mescaline and peyote a year ago and realizing from the inside-out that consciousness is a radically complex liberating concern beyond all political manipulation, his vision of the future had recently gained new shape and direction.

And so, while his friend Jonathan remained locked up during his first full day in jail, Stuart in his classy antique machine with its brand new Chrysler engine roared out of San Anselmo headed for Berkeley. As usual Stuart was not in the driver's seat. Like his dad before him, he preferred to be driven and today both Doug and Reggie had pushed for driver position. Douglas had managed to win out, leaving Reggie to slouch in the back.

The weather was quite bright outside the car but the prevailing atmosphere in the recently-reupholstered interior seemed slightly muffled as Douglas continued delivering his insider report on the committee meeting he'd attended that morning.

"Having the CIA show up there definitely clarifies the Establishment's intent in managing our scene," Doug was concluding. "And I say that right now we need to decide which way we ourselves want this 'Paul Unto Jesus' movement to flow – then we can define specific acts to help push things our direction. Is this your thinking, Stu?"

Half lost in entirely different thought flows, Stuart opined off the top of his head in his lofty mesmeric tone: "Like Bobby Zimmerman says over and over, nobody with any sense needs a Weatherman to know which way the wind blows – relax, Doug, I've got things all worked out already."

"Then why this trip to Berkeley to ask people what they think, if you've already got everything worked out?"

"Doug, psychic head's up – there's a basic rule of thumb in action here. Coordination always pays off – this shooting of the Christ figure somehow engages intimately with the larger notion of psychedelic warfare. Nothing is coincidence. No thing is coincidence. Get it? I mean really, get these lines: 'The new Christ drops LSD and begins preaching the Word – but then CIA agents extinguish the holy fire.' That'll make super hot press to totally counteract the Seminary line."

"Yeah," from Reggie in back. "Cool – perfect."

"Larry at the *Oracle*, he's our man. There's hundreds of student papers around the country that grab lead stories from them. It's the same with Patrice at Pacifica Radio – imagine a million students nation-wide hearing that the establishment just murdered the new revolutionary Jesus and is trying to cover it up. The next new assassination plot. If we play it right this situation'll set off explosions they can't never ever stop – especially if in the meantime we inundate twenty or thirty campuses with thousands and millions of tiny tabs from Jon's magic bottles."

"Oh by the way," Doug spoke up as they roared east around the top of the bay toward Oakland, "I went and talked to Jon in jail this morning. Just walked right in, no prob at all."

"What – you saw Jon?" from Reggie in back.

"Yes but to no avail. He stayed closed-mouth, hardly talked to me, at least not in there."

"Which was wise," Stuart reacted with a caustic bite. "Just like going there was totally unwise. I'm angry at you for acting without permission like that – dumbo!"

"So then," Doug retaliated, "why are we going over to meet with these Panther dudes and Weathermen and all the rest – that's not keeping mum. And they're on their own trips, not ours. Alan said stay totally clear of all that."

"Like I said, we go to listen lot and talk little. We're also set to smoke with the Brotherhood, chat about acid distribution. That's our mission today."

"Well shit," from the backseat, "like I suggested before, we should just pour it in the fuckin' Sacramento or even Washington water supply. Serious chemical warfare. Blow their fuckin' minds."

"Again the instant veto. And maybe it's best Jonathan's in jail right now – that was his original idea. Now we can act without dealing with that cowboy romance sop – besides it would dilute the supply to almost nothing. Run through the numbers, Reggie, why's everybody playing dumb here? Those four quarts work out to more than seven million trips at two-hundred mics a hit. The amount it takes to fly high can't even be seen by the naked eye – 200 micrograms is so totally tiny. Jon's acid, used properly, is our key to the future, it's going to be our activation button."

"You're assuming Jon told us straight," Doug spoke up, "that it's pure Sandoz, not already watered down."

"Paul told me he saw the bottles with his own eyes," Stuart assured him. "Formal printed labels in German and all the rest – CIA bought it direct from Sandoz in Zurich. MK-ULTRA to the hilt. Alan said that's been the story from the start, government fucking with people's minds. Joke's on them though – LSD is the liberator of us all."

"Ten bucks a hit," Reggie figured finally in his head, "that's fifty, hundred million bucks. No way we give all that acid free to the Brotherhood just to get it spread around fast. We did the hard work scoring it, we take a buck a hit for us. Split that down the middle, we're all rich."

"But this isn't about money," Stuart chided him.

"And let's not forget," Douglas said as he aimed the great rolling machine further down the American highway, "we don't have our hands on those bottles yet. If Jon stays in jail, there goes our liquid time-bomb right down the drain."

"But Julia must know," Reggie said. "What happened, Stu – you should'a pushed harder on her last night."

"She went nuts on me – bad timing."

"What'd you do, fuck her?"

"Shut your mouth. I don't know why I keep you around, the things you say."

"I had the connections, you were flying dry out here without me, don't forget that."

Silence reigned in the vehicle for a few miles as Stuart purposefully controlled his temper.

"Just assure me," Stuart went on calmly, "since we're on your turf over there, that all will go smooth today, no misunderstandings like last time."

"Hey, these dudes are brothers, man."

"Those guys are totally deluded low-mind Marxist pansies being played by the piper."

"Watch what you say."

Stuart turned fully around and looked Reggie in the eye. "One last time. Play this move just right – tell them we don't have the acid yet. Maybe we will soon but maybe we can't pull it off. Leave me an opening both ways."

"But how are we going to get the stuff, with Jon in jail?"

"Correct, Jon represents negative value behind bars. We therefore shall maneuver to free him."

"Oh sure, now we're bustin' people out of the clink like some two-bit movie."

"But of course, we shall employ a rather more suave manner of execution."

"So what's the plan, Mister Genius?"

"It's so simple you won't believe it."

13

Alan was running late for everything but he didn't care, he cancelled a lunch after the 11 o'clock lecture at City College, met for an important update with a shadow colleague, then drove fast all the way up to San Anselmo. Parking his VW bus just like he did last night, he stomped into the police station and demanded to talk with Jonathan Hadley.

The tough sexy cop wasn't there and the flow was effortless this time, very soon he found himself in a small interrogation room with Jonathan alive and mostly well walking into the room, flashing him a heated glance, sitting down onto the folding chair – then putting a small battery-run tape player on the metal table between them and cranking up some kind of hillbilly music that they had to talk over.

"My dad brought me that, earlier this morning," he explained. "Wise move."

"Ah. Well Jonathan – this is absolutely harsh. Every way. I came by last night but they didn't let me in"

"Katie told me."

"Katie?"

"Woman cop, she's okay, she knows I didn't do it but this is a nightmare, Alan – exactly the opposite of everything we expected or dreamed. Tell me what's happening, how can Paul be just suddenly dead?"

Alan sat there for three full breath cycles. "You're asking me yet another koan, Jonathan. Yes, why are we here? And why are you asking me that question?"

"I somehow can't focus on Paul's spirit – where is he, can you tune me into him or is he just – gone?"

"In the eternal unfolding of spirit into this sensory space-time continuum, Jon, I have no answers. I'm sitting here because I love you, I want to help."

"Well my dad's hot on the cop side, he's the best with that. But I'll give you a piece of the puzzle that might help. Something happened back at the Institute that got buried – and if I get locked up, maybe no one will ever find out so I need to tell you – but first you tell me. You and the Institute, you and the CIA. You and Tim – what's happening – did they kill Paul?"

"Another ultimate koan. You're seeking truth where there's nothing but ambiguity. Political shadow games – you have no idea how dark that shadow can get and I hope you never find out. No, I take that back. Always better to face it. Deal with reality."

"So – was that a yes?"

"There's so much I can't tell you, at least right now – and there's so much I myself don't yet know. I'm a pauper, a pawn, and so are you. Ants can't by definition perceive the tree they're crawling on. It's a wild west dynamics right now out here, there's no law and order at this level – no telling the good guys from the bad. We're all intermeshed and my allegiances far flung, you're not the only person in danger here. Speaking of which, what happened at the Institute?"

"Well – did you read the EEG research proposal that Bernie prepared and had me submit in my name?"

"Most of what Bernie and Humphry were doing wasn't run past me at all, I just came by to advise."

"Thing was," Jon said, "I thought that place was a safe haven. After Mom up and killed herself and all that, I thought we'd found a cure for mental problems, for my mom's depression attacks. Humphry seemed the genuine healer with his micro-dose psychedelic treatments – but then it all blew up in my face and now he's closed down and I'm in jail and the world's an entire fucked meaningless mess."

"So what did you want to tell me?" Alan pushed.

"No, you tell me first – specifically, were you getting paid by the Bureau Of Research In Neurology & Psychiatry – or by the CIA?"

"Jonathan. Please. Have you never been attracted to spy versus spy? Of course I can't tell you details of complex relationships, certainly not where I'm foresworn. Tell me what you have to say, and I'll do my best with the information. My heart feels good being here with you."

"What's scary is how something scientific and historical and important to the world can happen and then people can make that history just – disappear."

"History is nothing more than what second or third-hand witnesses choose to hold in their heads about stories that other people have concocted from sensory input and imagination and so forth – you're smart, you're a Princeton grad, you know all that. Tell me what was made to disappear, start at the beginning."

"Well I spent three years out there, getting more and more involved, working full time even before I graduated, it was challenging and draft-deferred and I was getting laid and paid, first as a subject and then Bernie graduated me to research hypnotist and then psychedelic guide. I was totally gung ho but then came the EEG study – by the way, my Psych advisor at Princeton, he knew all about it, he working for them too."

"Working for exactly whom?"

Jon looked right back at Alan across the metal divide of the desk. "Right after I tried to blow the whistle on the Institute for falsifying the LSD/EEG data, those two CIA ass-holes started hounding me, all the way out here. That's partly why my wife left me."

"Jonathan, we've already talked this through. The CIA was bothering you because when you left the Institute, several quarts of LSD mysteriously left the Institute that same day. The CIA considers that theft a potential act of terrorism – they'd definitely act on it."

"Okay – but what about Paul, you're the all-wise one, tell me – why would they kill Paul?"

"Who says they did?"

"You're the guru, you must know."

"I am not a fucking god."

"Well I'm fucking locked up in this jail for murder and maybe the murder has something to do with the Institute and that's what I'm asking you – does it?"

"I honestly don't know. There's a war going on throughout the world for the hearts and souls of the populace. America does have its secret service with tentacles in all our pockets. All we can do is dedicate our souls to striving for the higher good – even when we might temporarily run amuck and get stuck in CIA shit. So – back to the Institute, what's the story?"

"Just that Bernie falsified the EEG data from that LSD brain-damage research, and the tampered evidence of brain damage was released to the press and when I found out and blew my stack and threatened to expose what they'd done, all hell broke loose. That same night two CIA dudes showed up at my dorm room to scare me shitless and inform me that I was no longer employed at the Institute. That's when I phoned you, remember?"

"You never told me why you had to run."

"They said if I told anyone anything ever, they'd fucking kill me – just like that. Alan, America's being run by the new Gestapo and they assassinated Paul just like they assassinated the Kennedys and Martin Luther King and – "

"Easy, Jon. Life's a rough unfair game and who knows – I am still entirely in the dark regarding Paul but I know that every new moment determines the next moment. You are here in this jail cell, Paul is no longer with us except in spirit – you have a brilliant mind, you can move beyond all this, transfer to grad school at Stanford and carry on with your life work. I'm here to offer you a hand."

"But?"

"But I need you to tell me where those quart bottles are hiding. Once that's cleared up and behind you, I feel confident I can talk with people and deliver you from these gates of hell."

Jon sat looking over at the wiry little Englishman across from him. He inhaled slowly through the nose, exhaled – then slowly shook his head. "No, Alan. This just doesn't feel right."

"I know people, I can act to make things right between you and the government. The CIA assumes they're playing us but in fact we're playing them and I assure you, even when the path gets a bit devious or even heart-breaking, in the end we're going to win. Surrender the power in those magic bottles and you're off the hook."

"Alan, sorry – I'm running on gut feelings in here and right now my gut is saying a definite no."

14

Ty woke up with a start. Someone was prodding him with a stiff finger in his ribs. He came sitting up fast, reacting to the provocation – but a rough hand pushed him forcefully down again onto his back.

"Cool it Jacko," said a harsh male voice. "Ah, what do you have there?"

Ty in fact was holding a stuffed brown-paper bag in his hands, he'd been sleeping with it. His eyes blinked at the backlit male body hovering over him. The bedroom door was open – he was lying on Jonathan's bed where he'd retreated for a nap.

"So now just get yourself up on your feet nice and peaceful," the superior-sounding southern accent continued.

Ty sat up. The man in front of him had a pistol in his right hand. Ty nodded just slightly in acknowledgement. Caught in his stocking feet and feeling relatively naked without his boots and hat, he came passively to his feet. He noticed that his pistol and holster, which he'd left hanging from the bedpost, were missing.

The man in the suit flashed his ID in the relative darkness. "Agent Thomas," he said. "And you are Mister

Ty Hadley as per the name on the note we found on young Rupert's door – so what was that all about?"

"The boy was scared and good reason to be. Police brutality at a bare minimum – was that you kidnapping him off down to his room?"

"I wish it had been, they were a couple of new guys totally over-playing the assignment. You're lucky they didn't shoot you."

"Or me them. I'm DS, SLO. Where's my gun?"

"I know full well who you are. I asked you – why the posted note leading to this address?"

"The note was posted to put you on my scent and get you off Rupert's. He's done nothing."

"The note says you have the films – I assume that bag you're clutching is what I'm looking for."

"These films are evidence in a murder trial."

"I'm in a rush. Hand them over."

Ty hesitated, then tossed the bag fast and hard at the agent. Thomas almost dropped his gun trying to catch it.

"You're breaking the law and violating my rights," Ty informed him.

"My assignment is clear – to acquire and secure this evidence. You stole the evidence. Thus the gun."

"Well let's talk business," Ty offered. "My son's in jail for killing the guy on those rolls. He's innocent. Maybe there's information on the films that will help open up the investigation."

"There's something much bigger than a murder case here."

"And just what's bigger than murder?"

"Internal terrorism – with your beloved son right in the middle of the whole goddamn thing."

"And just where's your proof of that?"

"Alright then. Perhaps he didn't confide in you after all. Ten million hits of pure unadulterated Sandoz LSD was stolen from a federal research center several months ago by your very own very deviant kid. I intend to locate and re-possess that poison before it's used for terrorist purposes – which could be any moment now. So how about you be a law-abiding citizen and tell me where your boy's hiding the goods?"

"Hmm. Total blank slate on that one. How about you let me get my boots on?"

Thomas made a directional move with a wave of his pistol toward the living room. Ty grabbed his boots and walked out into brighter light. Julia was sitting there silently, another Fed watching her closely.

"Julie, you okay?" Ty asked her.

"They're thugs," she muttered. "I told them not to bother you."

"These guys are carefully trained to exhibit zero social skills. Don't pay them no mind."

He sat down on a chair and went to work pulling on his boots. Thomas settled on the sofa beside Julia, put the bag on the coffee table and started taking out the seven exposed but undeveloped rolls of Kodak film that Rupert had given Ty. Each roll was in an opened Kodak film box and each box had clearly-written dates and titles. Thomas lined them all in a row.

"So perf," he told his buddy. "Here we have three films of Professor Rosenblum's classes. The kid was shooting some documentary about the old guy which was why he had his camera rolling for this one, the first Jesus film: 'Paul Turns Into Jesus At Rosenblum Lecture.' How nice of him to make our work so easy."

"I do believe that's private property," Julia growled. "And you're in this house without a search warrant. I order you to leave immediately and leave the films behind – they're all I have left of my husband."

Thomas looked up at her a moment. He had dark brown eyes – somehow Julia'd assumed that all CIA agents were supposed to have steel blue eyes. "Young lady," he said to her evenly, "there's a war on, as you in particular well know since you sleep with the enemy. That means I have the power to do anything I damn well want in your little Communist cell here."

She looked to Ty. "Is that the truth?" she asked.

"Doesn't matter," he told her. "He's not playing by the rules – he's on some holy ego mission."

"I'm just in a major hurry," Thomas explained evenly, "short on time these days with five wildfires burning out of control in three cities. I'm due in Sacramento tonight so of necessity this is a rush job. And for the record what I'm doing here has nothing to do with ego – we're fighting to save this nation's ass and we deserve respect."

"Well I've worked side by side with several agents from your organization," Ty told him to his face, "who were top-notch and got my total respect. But you're off-base. You need to be hog-tied and pulled off this job."

"I fight to protect our country."

"I was brought up believing that the U.S. Constitution should never be violated, even when some sissy government officials piss in their pants. You're clearly breaking the law right now."

Thomas dropped the final rolls of film back into the bag. "So you're a lawyer, not just a two-bit rancher?"

"I went to college to study law."

"And what happened, country boy couldn't get his tiny rawhide mind around big city deals?"

"The war in Europe got hot and I went to fight –
for those same freedoms you're violating right now. I
might not agree with my son on a lot of things, but him
and his whole generation, they still have the God-given
American right to stand up and protest our government's
actions, whatever those actions might be. Your whole
Commie fear thing is just one more right-wing tactic –
there's no way this country's ripe ground for any
Communist take-over."

"You are so dense. My advice to you, cowboy, is
get out of town and stay out. The police will take proper
care of your son."

"And if you're done breaking laws for the
moment, you get your government asses out of here," Ty
told him right back.

"What about your son and those bottles of LSD
he stole? You have no idea how poisonous that stuff is,
millions of minds could be damaged. My colleagues lost
the trail for several months in New York but I'm back on
this case as of three days ago – and all roads lead right to
here."

"Well I'm no fan of illegal drugs, you can trust me
on that front."

"Mister Hadley, whether it's in chemical warfare
or trench warfare, I'd trust you about as far as I trust a
country weasel."

"Spoken like a true ol' southern rat."

"Some day you're gunna get yours."

"Meanwhile you watch your tail."

"Taylor, we're out'a here," he told his side-kick.

"Where are you taking those films?" Ty insisted.

"Some deep freeze."

"Use a fridge – you freeze 'em and they're
history."

"You don't even recognize sarcasm."

"I recognize justice being usurped under the faulty guise of phony terrorist fear-mongering."

"Hey, your son is a Communist sympathizer, Mister Hadley. Or worse. I do hope you feel proud. And speaking of Communists," he said, turning toward Julia. "what do you, you young lady of the left, know of those four bottles of poison – show me where they are and I'll get these films right back to you and find a way to get your lover boy our of lifer prison – I promise, your choice."

"I've no idea what you're talking about," she retorted.

Agent Thomas grinned his thin-lipped nasty snarl at her response, then turned back to Ty. "Here we have a perfect specimen of the law-abiding God-fearing young Americans you want to protect – playing innocent even while they lie to our faces and prepare to poison our minds. I gotta run but you bet, I'll be back."

He turned and walked quickly out, his lackey at his heels. Ty walked after the duo to make sure they were gone, shut the door with a slam and returned to Julia. For some reason he was suddenly grinning at her with obvious satisfaction.

"Well I must say, that went perfectly," he stated, quite pleased with himself.

She was up on her feet. "But – you just let them take the only evidence of Paul's teachings!"

"It's not quite like it looks – those were blank rolls that Rupert did up for me. I took the real rolls down to the police office before I came up here. So that's that. Now how about you and I go to the store for dinner supplies?"

"I already went to town while you slept."

"Hey, you're a dandy. Jon'll be lucky if he lands ya. By the way I'm pretty good with a peeling knife if you want to put me to work. I need something to do right now, aside from chase after that guy and get physical."

"That was amazing, how you took him on."

"I should have just sat back and let him walk away with the goods but he pushed my buttons."

"You must be thirsty. If you're anything like my Dad, you'd like a beer right around now. I bought Lucky, Coors, Bud and some German brand."

"A cold Bud would be dandy. No, I'll try the import. But tell me, just between you and me, do you know anything about all that LSD story?"

"No, no one told me anything – but I wouldn't be surprised if it was true."

"So you believe that Jonathan would commit an act of terrorism?"

She hesitated. "Everybody's throwing around that word at their enemies. And yeah, if you ask me, more and more people are getting so hot and bothered, angry and frustrated and blindly acting on their pet beliefs – who knows what they'll do next."

15

Kate meanwhile was up in her bedroom in her home way up in the high foothills of Mount Tam. Just emerging from a much-needed afternoon nap, she lay under the blanket with her eyes still closed and luxuriated in a slight stretch from her head to her toes and everywhere in between and suddenly she could feel that cowman's presence almost physically with her in bed – the body of that intelligent modern cowboy who had ridden into her life as a stranger and yet almost immediately seemed so similar to the missing lover she'd been imagining, dreaming, calling out to for so long now.

She slipped into memory and remembered him vividly, viscerally during their hallway encounter down at the police station: You must have antennas, she'd said to him … just one … you're not talking dirty to me are you … not yet … How could that kind of conversation happen between two people who'd just met, she asked herself. How could time get so compressed that six hours felt like six weeks? And how come she was feeling seventeen again, barely touched, never ever really touched like she wanted to be touched ...

For an unrequested moment she remembered her husband Claude telling her that she was frigid because she didn't want him to touch her anymore. But of course he'd been the frigid one – dick as cold as ice when it came to emotions. After the wild honeymoon fling was over she'd step by step realized that Claude mostly wanted somebody like her just for a quick fuck and then he went right back to his compulsive work which was in the end nothing less than a constant rampage of quasi-legal economic rape and corporate pillage.

Paul had been speaking about all that, his insights into the world situation had been so lucid. In fact Kate had recently found herself agreeing more and more with what the kids over at Berkeley were shouting – that it's the adults who're out of control and violating society by making filthy money killing people ten thousand miles away who'd never even attacked America in the first place. Claude was a sicko corporate robot with no sense of real morals at all. In the end she'd been ashamed to be his wife – and she was still working on her secret investigation to expose him.

She got up from bed in underwear and reached for her regular lady-cop slacks, then remembered that this evening was a social dinner, not work. What would Ty Hadley be like when they weren't playing police games? Paul had said something yesterday in his last talk – something about learning to trust and genuinely open up and surrender to being who we really are and becoming utterly honest with each other about what we really need and desire in life ...

That young man's inspired voice was still in her ears, he'd shared so many resonating insights that'd penetrated her heart, ancient spiritual truths expressed in a radical new way. He hadn't acted as if he was playing Jesus like people tried to in the movies – he'd actually been fully himself and yet ... for the first time she felt hit with a gripping panic and horror – what if Paul had in fact somehow been the new Jesus, what if society had killed their savior yet again?

She threw that entire thought out of her mind and pulled her focus back to her job of finding that young man's killer. She should have brought professionals in from some other police jurisdictions to help her in the investigation but somehow, right from the first, there had been a resistance to doing that, to going into manic cop gear with this case. And then Ty appearing had further shifted her attitude – the two of them could handle this case on their own.

Looking by rote through her closet for something sexy, she realized it'd been not weeks and months but years since she'd felt like this, wanting to dress up for a man. After the divorce there'd never been anyone who'd made her want to swirl her skirt and flash with female desire. Now though – but this was ridiculous. Cool it, Detective – act your age. And it's only four o'clock, you have time for one or two interviews before the dinner so – dress soberly.

In the end she chose a sleek burgundy dress she'd had for years but never felt quite ready to show off her stuff in. She tossed it on the bed, stepped out of her underwear and into the shower, doing her best not to hope for too much.

Down in town, within an entirely divergent reality in the San Anselmo Presbyterian Church manse, Stella was in the kitchen preparing a special quiche she knew Wilma just loved. From Stella's perspective there was no reason at all for Wilma to continue being so terribly upset and irritable – someone had now been arrested and locked up in jail for the murder of that poor deluded seminary boy.

All was calm and in order, Wilma could have a delicious dinner with plenty of wine and then she would reconnect with her more tender feelings and they would lock all doors and rediscover each other anew.

She carried a tray of tea into the study as was customary at 4:20 sharp during the winter months, just as the light was beginning to fade outside in the garden. Hot tea and crumpets, sometimes buttered scones prepared exactly like Wilma's mother had prepared them back in Foxen Place. The small but brightly-crackling oak fire was softly roaring as Stella came walking into the study – but Wilma was still in her adjoining office and the door was closed.

She put down the tray, nervous about disturbing Wilma but also afraid not to serve the afternoon tea on time. She was just approaching the door to the office to rap ever so quietly, when she heard the chimes of the front door. She tensed, knowing that no one was expected and that the entire community knew never to disturb the Reverend in her home without previous appointment.

In her office Wilma heard the chimes as well. Her head snapped up. She had been sitting with her Bible in her lap, seeking solace but finding none – she must have dropped off to sleep because the big wall clock showed 4:22 and the last time she'd looked it had been 3:47. She had slept hardly a wink last night, not to mention the night before. She stood up, her bones stiff and joints painful, and was limping toward the door when there was a light rap.

"Come in," she intoned, her voice flat from disuse.

And just like that, in walked Stella with a very racy-looking young lady wearing a red dress that really had no place in decent society.

"I'm so sorry to disturb you," Stella stuttered, "but this woman is from the police and she insists on speaking with you."

"Oh, do you?" Wilma said at the woman, feeling suddenly shaky and hot. "Then you can do as everyone does and phone my secretary at the office."

She turned around to walk away.

"When a community breeds murder," the young police woman said right back, "there's no time to waste on formalities. I ask you to cooperate with your police force in this matter. I need to talk with you, time is of the essence."

Wilma stopped, turned around. "But I was led to believe that you captured your murderer and have him under lock and key."

"We've detained a suspect but there are details which must be clarified immediately."

"I read about you in the paper – you're the detective who was hired several months ago. Something about difficulties in the City."

"There was a disagreement among professionals. I chose to remove myself from the disagreement." She took her shield out of her matching velvet purse. Wilma took the small wallet in her own hands, inspected the identification closely.

"So then," Wilma spoke tersely to Stella who was standing anxiously to the side, "it appears that tea is to be disrupted by a government official who must currently be wearing a disguise – what is it you are disguised as tonight, a hooker perhaps?" she fired at Kate.

"This will take just ten minutes," Kate said, not rising to the bait.

"Well then go into the study. I'll make a phone call and join you in a moment. "

She turned and walked stiffly away, arthritic pain in her left hip causing the limp. Kate followed Stella into the parlor where Kate sat and Stella busied herself nervously with the tea things but never met Kate's eyes.

"So, did you happen to hear any of the talks that Paul Jacobs gave before he was killed?" Kate asked her.

"Me? Oh no. No."

"You seem upset about something."

"Upset? No."

"Do you live here?"

"Upstairs. Yes."

"Were you here Sunday evening?"

"Sunday? Of course."

"The two of you were here together?"

"My my," Wilma said from the doorway, "you are the intrepid detective. Stella please serve tea."

Stella served and then backed away and out of the room. The remaining two women sat in silence facing each other across an inlaid antique coffee table.

"Alright then," Wilma finally intoned, putting down her cup and saucer and glaring at Kate. "How might I help your steamy little investigation?"

Kate put down her cup, took out her note pad and pen. "Did you know the deceased, Paul Jacobs?"

"I knew that he was among that ruffian group that came to the Seminary in this year, the druggies."

"When was he specifically brought to your attention?"

"When was it, Saturday – he was giving one of his ridiculous talks and several of my parishioners suggested I go listen."

"Why would they suggest that?"

"Because he was speaking heresy and hogwash on our Seminary campus. I naturally need to stay abreast of such developments."

"I see."

"Oh do you?"

Kate smiled back demurely into the older woman's scowl. "How many times following that first encounter were you in the young man's presence?"

"Well he had the audacity to appear at my Sunday morning worship service."

"And what happened?"

"Why, he barged in with an unruly flock of hippie admirers and virtually took over my church, forcing me to finally step aside and allow him to preach his filthy nonsense."

"You sat quietly and listened?"

"Only for a few painful minutes – then I took the liberty of turning my back and walking out on him. You must understand, he was speaking heresy against the Church."

"So you were angry at him?"

"I most certainly was – and rightly so!"

"Was that Sunday morning the last time you saw him before he was murdered?"

"Most definitely."

"But you perhaps heard reports of his further activities that day?"

"I had several people monitoring his every word and recording him on tape as well."

"I'll need to copy those recordings at your earliest convenience. Where are they?"

"I ordered them destroyed."

"Interesting – why would you do that?"

"The man was dead, after all – there was no need to preserve his blasphemous rantings."

"I see."

"I doubt that very much. You strike me as someone with their own private agenda – I wonder what it is. Surely you're not another deluded follower of that maniac."

"I am a police officer investigating his murder."

"I'm really quite tired of all this, are you finished?"

"I received a report that on Sunday night, the night of the shooting, you attended a private meeting of concerned Seminary and church leaders at the Administration building."

"Indeed."

"What was the purpose of that meeting?"

"We were discussing how to deal with our dilemma."

"What plans did you generate?"

"I'm afraid I'm not at liberty to discuss that meeting without permission from the President of the Seminary, he was the one who called the meeting."

"And looking back, where were you from eleven that evening to midnight?"

"Oh my, now we're being very dramatic."

"A simple answer will suffice."

"How dare you!"

"It's my role to ask that question of a great many people, Ma'am."

"Don't Ma'am me. I came directly from that meeting, at around ten-twenty, to my house here. Stella can vouch for me, we had a sandwich in the kitchen I remember, just after eleven, and then retired upstairs."

Kate stood up.

"Tell me," Wilma asked. "Where is the body, what are they doing with Paul's body?"

"At the deceased's parents request it's to be cremated tomorrow morning, and the ashes flown back to a memorial service in New York."

"Cremated? You mean physically destroyed?"

"Basically, yes."

"Oh God. That is rather final. Aren't his believers crying out in anguish and complaining?"

"Complaining about what?"

"But of course – if he was perhaps the true second coming of Christ, won't cremation destroy any chance of his physical resurrection from the dead?"

"I have no idea. Theology's not my area of expertise," Kate said back to her curtly. "I am looking for a murderer, not a savior."

Kate made her exit from the house into the chill of late afternoon sunlight, having chosen not to butt heads further for the time being with the minister. She closed the door behind her and took three steps down into the front garden and ran right into a man in a suit.

"Excuse me," he said in a southerly accent. "Are you the local police woman here to interview the minister?"

"And who might you be?"

"Agent Thomas Quill." He flashed his ID. "I have only a moment, can we talk?"

"Wilma phoned you?"

"Correct."

"What on earth does she have to do with the CIA?"

"Nothing really, except proximity to a situation. I'm connected with the Jacobs murder and several extenuating circumstances which include national security and possible terrorist activity. I just want to touch base with the local police and let you know I'm in your neighborhood. I request that you contact me immediately if any new developments are unearthed in this case. Here's my card."

Kate took it, looked him hard in the eye – but could tell nothing at all. "I've found no security issues. So what can you tell me about the case?"

"Nothing so far – of necessity, confidentiality reigns. What I'm requesting is that you go very carefully about the investigation. You already have the probable murderer. I need you to keep the case simple so that you don't muddy the larger pond I'm working."

"I see."

"Good then – I've got to run now, I should be back sometime tomorrow. If you come across anything at all new on this case, call that number any time day or night – you do understand by law that this is now your responsibility. Anything at all new, you phone me. And don't bother Wilma any further, she's upset but she's clean."

Without further ado the man turned on his heel and walked quickly out the garden path to the street where a car and driver awaited.

16

Exiting the Oakland freeway in order to get onto the upper-bay Novato road that ran westward across the marshlands, Douglas was once again at the wheel of the old sedan because Reggie had recently inhaled a bit too much on a communal pipe whereas, as usual, Douglas had not.

Spirits of the threesome were high – even Stuart was visibly pleased, sitting in the passenger seat leaning back and quietly gazing at a winter sunset exploding over the coastal heights of Mount Tamalpais to the west.

"That was just so fuckin' cool," from Reggie in back, emerging from a blissful interlude of smoky silence. "Like they were falling all over us, you guys saw that? They want the goods and we're like coming to them at a quarter price their usual acid man and hey, we're still going to make our holy buck times four million I mean, split three ways that's just fuckin' groove."

"I told you not to get stoned on this trip," Stuart said back to him, with an edge to his voice.

"Well and you insulted them, man, like here we are talking the biggest deal ever and you won't even smoke with the brothers."

"Whatever. I now have in hand our required outflow link. So let's refocus – on getting those films that guy shot of Paul, that's now top priority. If we're going to have them out playing on campuses everywhere in the whole country by next week, we've got work. Doug, as soon as we get back you're going to head over to that kid Rupert and get the films from him one way or the other, right?"

"Hey," from Reggie again, "I'm in on that too."

"You're too fucked up – you're out."

"Bull to that, you can't just bump me."

"Doug, do you want Reggie going with you on that assignment?" Stu asked his driver, who was focused maneuvering like a former jet pilot naturally would, aviator glasses in place against the last rays of sun.

"No way do I want him with me."

"Get off it," Reggie complained from the back. "I mean, I can fly a fucking jet this high."

"You're buggin' me," Stuart told him curtly. "Any more of this shit and you're gone."

"Oh sure, you're going to drop your hook with the Brotherhood and lose four mill."

Stuart didn't respond. Douglas eyed Reggie in the rear-view mirror – then returned his focus to the driving, it was rush hour, Monday traffic heading back to Marin County. "So phone me later," Stuart told Doug. "You sure you don't need me?"

"That guy's a wimp, I know how to play him."

"Maybe don't come up tonight, I have to handle Dana and all the rest."

"You going to talk to Jon?"

"Are you kidding, show my face there?"

Doug eyed him a moment, then returned his attention to the road. "What – you think they suspect you?"

"The wise move like Farina told us, is to stay invisible. Stick your neck in the noose even for a second and they just might pull. We know what we're after – we want Jon out. It's what we do after he's out that's key. So stay clear of him in the meantime."

"Whatever you say, boss."

"You being sarcastic?"

"No, Stu. Just trusting you, that's all."

"You're not like Reggie are you, panting after bucks rather than sticking to the higher cause?"

"You know me better than that."

"Tell you the truth, Doug, I don't know you hardly at all, you're not exactly talkative about your past."

"Ask away then."

"I was naturally wondering what actually happened to you, that gave you the limp and all."

Doug drove in silence for a few breaths. "You want details? It happened fast. We were at a thousand feet moving in for a drop around dusk – something from the left hit us and we exploded and I ejected and some time later, I was mostly unconscious, a chopper picked me up. My buddy, they never found him."

"What about your conversion experience, turning coat on the government?"

"I was talking with some guys in the hospital and listening to a couple Vet protesters and it just started making sense, that's all. Ever since then it's just been the flow, you know – all I had to do was see the light, realize who the real bad guys were, swallow my pride and join the other side. It's been a wild ride."

"You don't smoke, don't drop – straight lace."

"I like a clear head. Like Baez and Seeger keep saying, too much drugs can ruin a movement."

"Alan says we don't want a movement."

"And Alan's God?"

"Alan's just Alan."

"Hey, I just want that war to stop, Stu. I'm committed to the cause just like you. You're more on top of all this so you're the boss – that's all I'm saying."

Stu eyed him. "Okay then. I didn't mean to give you trouble."

"Hey," Reggie interjected from the back. "You guys fuckin' won't believe who I ran into when you two were so busy with the business rap."

"What you talking about?" Stu asked.

"I just went to pee and there was my cousin Tanya that I went to high school with and get this, she works in the fuckin' cafeteria part time at the state capital in Sacramento, I mean, is that like Allah's hand in all this or what – and she said definitely, she'd blow their minds, she could like without any prob at all slip half a cup of our super stuff into the soup or the coffee or whatever next week, totally blast the whole California government into space, man – I mean she said she'd really do it, we're like in place to bomb the fucking shit out of the government, like I just ran into her in the hallway and it just like happened, hand of fuckin' God in all of this."

Stuart was listening, staring ahead but not seeing the sunset anymore. He didn't respond when Reggie fell silent. Nor did Doug. Instead they looked across at each other a moment, then continued staring ahead.

"Look at that fuckin' sunset," intoned Reggie from behind.

And indeed, it was fuckin' glorious.

17

Ty right then could see the same sunset, but over in his view it was shining softly through the slightly-swaying boughs of the redwoods out the back window of Jon's cottage. He had a knife in hand that Julia had found for him and he was slicing and sawing and chopping away at various proffered veggies with a carpenter's strength, precision, pleasure.

"Must be in the genes," he said to Julia as she stirred a cream sauce atop the old gas stove. "I just like cutting, whacking, slicing, trimming, all this general kind of work."

"The good husband helping in the kitchen."

"I don't know – after the fact you can always look back and wish you'd done more."

"She's been gone how long?"

"Nine, ten years."

"No one new?"

"Oh, a neighbor came over quite a lot after Loretta was gone, cooking me some nice dinners, filling the freezer with casseroles. Her Hank died and she was lonely and pretty but I just wasn't much in the market. When you really love somebody you're not looking right away for replacements."

"Now you make me feel guilty, how I shifted sort of fast from Paul to your Jonnie."

"No, I didn't mean – sorry."

"But I'd left Paul in my heart a long time ago. Not in your kind of time frame, but that one year with Paul seemed forever. In the beginning he'd been mostly constantly fun and funny, lovey dovey and all the rest – but then I started to notice more and more times when he was way withdrawn into himself, caught up in intense feelings but so distant from me, then turn again into real kind and loving – but way too often, since we moved out here, he either wasn't present for me at all, off in his wild mystic dream worlds, or he'd shift into his, well, his other very much less pretty personality."

Ty's fingers had been working with knife and onions, his eyes staying on the job. Now he paused, looked up at the young woman he was sharing kitchen space with. She was almost tall, slender with curly black hair and she sported a slight sensual slackness to the lips as if, right under the surface, a whole bunch of thoughts and emotions were on the verge of busting forth.

"You mentioned chopping, sawing," Julia was saying. "Reminds me – every autumn my little brother, myself, my dad and his brother would go camp in the higher hills, New York has some hills you know. We'd settle into some forest and saw, saw, saw – get the winter wood in."

She took the onions, carrots. celery and cabbage he'd chopped according to her general specifications and tossed them into her pan of garlic and olive oil. The roast was starting to smell good in the oven and she'd whipped up an old-fashioned apple pie, done a bit different than he was used to, which stood ready to pop in the oven as soon as the roast came out.

"So you're a country girl," he said.

"Dad had the farm but he liked working with wood so much, he converted one of the barns into a little furniture factory." She wiped her eyes with the back of her white shirt sleeve, remembering for a moment. "I loved it, out there on the farm, but I ended up leaving even before I quit high school. Later on I studied art history at NYU with a specialty in my dad's favorite period, seventeenth-century European furniture. Right now I'm apprenticed to an amazing furniture designer, Karl Rubens down in Mill Valley. My Dad and I though, we still don't speak."

"Why's that?"

She paused and looked him in the eyes. There were tears glistening suddenly. She sniffled. "Sorry," she said.

"Talk if you like, sometimes it helps."

She reached, sipped her glass of wine on the counter, put it back down. "My uncle was staying alone with me one weekend out at the farm, it was the Fair and I didn't want to go. I'd just turned sixteen. He started drinking, and, well – he just took me. Twice the first day, then again Sunday morning before everybody got home. Said he'd kill me if I told, that I was all to blame, always asking for it."

She stopped, pushed loose hair away from her eyes. "After that I was a mess, flunking where I'd always been top of my class. The counselor knew something was wrong and got me to confess. My whole family turned on me when the police came, my Dad especially. I just got on a Greyhound and went all the way down to the City, an aunt took me in. But you see, sometimes when Paul was drinking and being rough with me, I'd react like he was my uncle, I'd suddenly want to – inside my heart, I felt like I could murder him."

She was microscopically shaking with emotion. Ty walked close and put an arm around her. They heard a knock – she gasped for breath, he removed his arm.

"Well – thanks," she said, her voice raspy. "I don't know why – that just had to come out."

Ty went off without much forethought through the living room with candles burning and fire crackling in the fire place, his mind still intensely focused on that sudden revelation from Julia. When he opened the door there stood Kate –

She looked hardly recognizable, some kind of fantasy movie star in that knock-out sleek dress and her hair all down and flying around her utterly beautiful bare shoulders. Plus the look in her eyes – the look was wild like a high-strung wilderness animal ready to break and run at the very least sign of danger.

"Oh Lordy," was all he could mutter.

"What – something wrong?"

"I'm lookin' at some angel and you talk about something wrong?"

"Damn, so I'm overdressed."

"You're so darn flesh beautiful you took my breath clean away. Julie, she's something else. And now you about double. I feel like a dumb ugly cowpoke."

He stepped aside as she came walking in but she fooled him and walked right into his arms rather than on into the room. That wasn't her plan, it was simply what her body chose to do right then – ground out in him, get her arms all the way around and pull him right against her just for that one moment. Then she pushed back, bashful, walking fast away and into the kitchen to greet Julia.

Ty found himself almost instantly at the door again, welcoming the two other guests for the evening. Norrie Rosenblum was the variety of mother-hen you wished would set up nest close by so you could enjoy her special mix of concern and compassion on a regular basis. She was even shorter than the Professor, whom she called Bernie Dear, and not a skinny girl by any means.

She went floating into the kitchen without hesitation, gave Kate a formal handshake and Julia a good long hug. It seems Julia had helped her in her kitchen a few weeks ago, so they agreed to settle in together to finish up preparations – but first, Kate brought a bottle and glasses of wine to Ty and the professor in the living room. Bernie seemed somewhat subdued, sitting quietly, mostly staring into the fire. Ty couldn't figure out the old man's emotions, they were distant, edged a bit with some hostility that seemed unrelated to the present circumstances. He sipped on his wine just twice, grunted at a couple of friendly questions Kate offered him, then retreated into fire gazing.

Ty glanced at Kate and she glanced back at him and he glanced away to the fire and she told herself that this was ridiculous, trying to control an urge to just grab this guy's hand and drag him into the bedroom and close the door and jump ahoy. She was both embarrassed and confused by feeling such raw emotions but she couldn't put the inner flame out. In fact her body felt so afire that the fire itself made her too hot – so she stood up and walked off down the hallway to the back of the house.

The back-porch door was slightly ajar, its jam smashed in from outside. She remembered the break-in just this morning in this same house when Julia had been sleeping alone in that bedroom. Damn, who had that been? There had been so many differing fingerprints – she pushed the door open and stepped out onto the back porch where a three-quarter moon was already up, a towering stand of redwoods casting moon shadows so black that the eye could hardly penetrate them down close to the ground.

The chill air did bring her suddenly back to her senses and then normal thoughts cut in again. A remarkable young man had been murdered right next door just the night before. Another young man was in jail for the murder and he almost certainly hadn't done the murdering. So – where was that real killer right now? There were half a dozen people she could already name, one of whom might be the killer but thusfar there was absolutely nothing concrete pointing anywhere particular. Total blank.

She got caught up for a moment feeling guilty for taking the evening off rather than pushing deeper into the case. Ty's voice jolted her suddenly from behind: "Might I intrude?"

She spun around. He was standing there just a few feet from her on the small rickety porch, a touch of moonlight half-catching his face. "You're quiet in those boots," she said.

"Sometimes. By the way, I checked down below – there's a back path down there, a short cut to a residential road a hundred yards down that comes up from near the gate and dead-ends at three faculty houses on the side of the hill."

"Yes, I know," she told him.

"Those steps over there from Paul's back door, they go down to the same trail – anyone could have come up the path, done the shooting and then ran back down to a waiting car or over to the lower dorms, or over the wall."

"That would explain how Jon walked into the house but found no shooter," she concluded. "I have those houses on my list for tomorrow morning."

"Want me to go do it right now?"

She looked up at him in the moonlight. "Maybe for Julia's sake we don't play police tonight. That's why I agreed to this dinner – for her sake. It was thoughtful of you to suggest it."

"So tell me – who's on top of your suspect list?"

"I've never felt so blank," she admitted. "My instincts are usually hot but this case – maybe there's some maniac like you said who felt compelled to kill the AntiChrist. Maybe some hood from New York cruised into town, did his dirty work and left. There's the slight possibility that Dana did it, jealous women sometimes do the unthinkable. I interviewed the local minister and even she makes me suspicious, still spitting hatred at Paul's violation of her deepest beliefs. Otherwise there's an entirely unknown killer out there this very moment packing who knows what motives."

"Yeah, and I hate to say it," he told her. "but Julia told me that she herself sometimes wanted to kill Paul. It came out of her like a geyser, she couldn't stop it."

"No – not Julia. But I have no idea where to push, where to dig. I guess that's why I'm here tonight doing nothing. Just standing here. No movement."

And so they stood there not moving, looking into each other's eyes. Hardly breathing. Unable to look away or talk shop, unable to talk at all. Ty felt his focus slip entirely away from his son and the murder as his senses and heart fixated on the live feminine presence of the woman, not the detective, standing so close looking up into his eyes like she was some sudden ignited goddess.

"Uhm – maybe we should just go back in," he finally managed to say in a gravelly voice.

"What now – you're afraid of me?"

"Afraid of myself more than you."

"Same here. Nobody but nobody makes me feel this way," she told him, almost feeling angry at how her breathing was changing and how she felt weak in the knees and embarrassingly eager to just find a place right now to surrender to the languid entirely pull of gravity and get horizontal. "It's unprofessional, this has got crazy between us and you know it."

"I know it. I just can't stop it."

"Big strong man like you."

"Totally beguiling woman like you."

"So I'm beguiling, am I?"

She was gazing up into his eyes in the moonlight as the kiss began almost in slow mo – they quite honestly felt under some spell, unable to stop themselves even though it was most definitely totally inappropriate behavior. At first they were just leaning slightly into each other, breathing together, feeling the vibrant solidity of each other. Hungry fingers reached out and around all on their own and in the blind process of running those fingers lightly all up and down and all over her various silk-covered backside curves Ty discovered no sign of bra nor underwear at all while meanwhile she was discovering that indeed his rough cowboy lips tasted so good she wanted to consume him for dinner and suspected that his bulging pressure against her own middle erogenous zones was seriously contemplating the possibility of rummaging her right then and there in the steamy moonlight.

By the time they finally managed to gasp in unison and break free from each other she knew she had to have him all the way – it was intellectually crazy but it was erogenously the most real thing either of them had felt for – well, for way longer than they would admit.

"Please, come on up to my place," she said to him bluntly. "Afterwards – will you?"

"Uhm yeah – but hear me out right now – we need to concentrate, I've planned something. We've got a shooter to catch, maybe right here tonight in a make-do trap baited for around nine-thirty, ten at the latest because just as soon as it looks like we've all left the cottage except for Julia, I've got this feeling some vermin might show up. I need some definite break on all this. And you gotta help."

18

"Stella!"

No answer from upstairs.

"Damn you, Stella, get down here – right now!"

The office door opened and innocent Stella stood there aghast at what she saw – her staid employer, her secret lover, her only true friend in life sitting there across the room slouched on the sofa, a bottle of who knows what and a half-full glass of it on the coffee table in front of her, the bottle mostly empty. Could that be whiskey? The smell was foul in the room.

"Stop staring at me – so I'm drinking. Probably drunk. Didn't you ever see somebody drunk before?"

"No. I mean yes. My father. But never you."

"I want you to pack and get out of this house right now, this very moment. I want you out in ten minutes."

"But Wilma – "

"Don't But Wilma me, out, out! This is my house, I've a right to get drunk in my own house, and I have every right to order you out. So out!"

"But – why? What have I done to – "

"It's not what you've done, idiot. It's what I've done."

"And what have you done?"

"Crucified my Lord – crucified my Lord!"

"Of course you haven't – "

"You know nothing, you're a dumb blank slate – wake up, Stella! You play like you're deaf and dumb and innocent as the virgin lamb but we both know what you really are – and you know what has happened."

"No, I don't. I don't!"

"The Lord's body has been plunged into an infernal flame and forever destroyed before it can arise – look at what we have done!"

"But you said yourself that – "

"You know as well as I do that most of what I say is pure slop. I've been a wonton whore for the Church and the Church has rejected our Lord. And now I'll burn forever."

"Paul Jacobs was the AntiChrist, you yourself said that he – "

"Shush. Just shut your mouth. Now."

"But I can't just – "

Wilma burst suddenly into an explosion of sobs. She swooped with her hand wildly in front of her and knocked the whiskey bottle down onto the expensive Persian rug but she didn't care any more – about anything. After so many years of contrite devout self-control she was now entirely out of control, making drunken animal sounds of both agony and outrage.

With great bravery Stella came around the coffee table to try and touch her, comfort her – but Wilma was not to be comforted. "Away from me!" she shouted, standing up dizzily and glowering at her friend. "I told you to leave this house immediately, this has nothing to do with you. Get out while you can – pack a bag and call a taxi, you have your bank account – go anywhere, I don't care, but get out!"

Stella was entirely aghast and helpless at this point. "Wilma, surely you can't be serious."

"I am much worse than serious, I am deadly, I am among the condemned and I will not tolerate your continued presence – out with you!"

"No, I won't leave you in this condition!" Stella shouted back in defiance, her thin voice cracking with fear and emotion.

"Then you will surely go down with me."

Wilma went walking fast on wobbly bare feet over to her desk, collapsed down into the swivel chair, slid open a drawer – and came out with a .22 pistol in her hand. She pulled back the hammer and aimed.

"So then – I said out," she muttered in a different low menacing voice.

"Wilma, you stop this – put that down!"

In response, almost instantly thereafter the pistol cracked loudly with a sudden deadly explosion of ignited gun powder.

19

The small dining-room table just managed to hold all five of them. Wine was flowing and the roast disappearing fast. A couple of times, memories of previous dinners at this table made Julia look like she was going to break down and cry again, which would have been entirely understood – but each time she blinked back tears and came through like a champ, even managing to carry on a fairly coherent hostess conversation with her guests.

"I took a nutrition course at NYU," she was saying halfway through the roast and scalloped potatoes, "and I found out that it takes around six pounds of grain to produce just one pound of meat. The professor hit us with the statistic that if most Americans cut down on meat and dairy just ten percent, and the feed-grain saved went instead to the hundreds of millions of people going hungry and starving to death around the world, every human being could go to sleep every night with their stomachs full. So mostly now I'm cutting down on meat – but I must admit, this is good."

"Well I hope you're not going to put us cattle ranchers entirely out of business," Ty responded. "We treat our cattle about as good as could be – but yeah, I read the same statistics myself. My wife was reading all those books and now, with her gone, I still sit most evenings and read 'em, kind'a keeps me in touch with her."

He fell silent a moment, glanced over at the two elderly folk at the table. Norrie was listening intently but the old man was staring blankly at food mostly uneaten on his plate.

"I'll tell you the real culprit," Ty went on. "Back in the fifties America had a giant surplus of corn and soy beans so the government upped its beef grading system. There was no dietary logic to it but all of a sudden we had to treat our already perfectly-tasty grass-fed cattle to three months of feedlot grain in order to get top grading and make a profit. Ain't that how it always seems to go – big government panders to special interests, meanwhile people starve."

"But your government here is so much better than what I grew up with in Poland," Norrie interjected. "You must always work to preserve your freedoms."

"I agree with that," Kate interjected, and then turned to look to the Professor. "So, I hear that you knew Paul," she ventured.

He at first didn't seem to have heard. Then he slowly glanced her way with a wary look. "Yes, that is true," he said with his European accent. "I knew the boy quite well before his breakdown. Perhaps, if I am honest, I am afraid I might be responsible for what happened."

"Now Bernie dear," Norrie interjected.

"Please – what do you mean?" Kate pushed him.

He stared back at her a long moment, his eyes like a Beagle's, full of emotion – then without speaking further he turned his head and looked off across the small dining room to the fire in the living room.

"Perhaps I can explain," Norrie spoke up, her voice nervous. "Ever since he heard this morning of the shooting he has been like this, caught in guilt. In the last few decades but more after we moved here from New York, Bernie has been, well – different sometimes. Shifting into unexpected moods. For considerable time it was a blessing, especially when teaching the Old Testament prophets – he will stand in front of his class and become entirely silent, focusing inward upon a particular Biblical character. Then he begins quoting exact words which that prophet spoke – and suddenly he slips into a special state, perhaps you would call it an actor's trance. He begins speaking in a different voice altogether, as if he has actually become that historic person."

"That boy Rupert with the camera," Ty said, "he told me he was filming the professor doing just that."

"Yes, I know Rupert," she said.

"Oh – how is that?"

"Recently I accompanied Bernie to his lectures. He still drives but sometimes gets confused. And you see, this is what has him so upset – Paul watched him many times as he changed right before his eyes into Jonah, Jeremiah, Moses, Elijah. Then, under the influence of that mind-altering drug it seems that Paul himself changed, but into Jesus Himself – and then failed to pop out of the spell like Bernie always does, thank God. Who knows, maybe Bernie won't pop out some day."

She herself fell silent at that point.

"I've read some theological books recently," Ty spoke up to fill the silence. "There's this German fellow Dietrich Bonhoeffer who writes about trusting God to act through you – trusting your spiritual instinct to do good. He himself was right out there trying to knock off Hitler, power to him."

"Yes, yes," from Bernie, who was again listening.

"So can you tell me," Ty asked him, "from your experience is it possible for God or Christ or whatever, the real thing now, not just the idea – for God to actually speak through a regular human being?"

The table was quiet. Bernie exhaled loudly, then again turned and stared off at the fire across the room – then slowly turned his scraggly head of white hair and looked to his wife, then back to Ty. "Before the war and my conversion into Christianity I was a Jewish theologian for many years," he told the table, "lost entirely in thought. But I became possessed with doubt and one night suddenly I felt I would die, that the Devil was coming for me – and right then I opened up and there was Christ in the flesh before me. I actually felt God's touch on the back of my neck, a burning tingling sensation."

He stopped talking again, drifting off.

"Bernie dear," his wife encouraged, "can you tell us what happened then?"

He turned his head, looked at her and snapped back into lucidity. "Yes, well. I had of course read the passage in Acts where Holy Spirit comes rushing into the room filling the hearts and minds of the disciples. That night in New York something similar happened to me – there came out of nowhere this great roaring in my ears and then the sense of being penetrated, being pierced by Christ Himself – directly in my heart."

He dropped into silence, his gnarled hand holding his wine glass shaking so much that the red liquid sloshed around inside.

"So do you think," Ty asked quietly, "that Jesus could have been talking to us directly through Paul?"

The old man seemed struck in the face with the words. He sat up rigidly and glowered at Ty. "Absolutely not!" he reacted, his voice becoming louder, as if from a distant impersonal source. "It is true, we all must welcome God to speak and act through our mortal bodies – this is our primary spiritual duty as Christians, to let God act – we must not question, we must not falter on the path! Show me where I end and where my God begins, I challenge you! There is no boundary between the human and the divine … but open your ears now. Paul violated the sacred veil. This LSD drug – that chemical is the Devil in action, do not forget the Devil! Paul was without question taken over by the Devil. The bible says God is love but also that God is the wielder of truth's almighty sword! Our God is eternal, infinite, and totally beyond judgment – and his acts likewise. Amen and again – amen."

The fire crackled. The old man glared intensely at each of the members of the table – then stood up with considerable power, a wild look in his eyes. But right then something happened, he seemed to shrink, lose his focus. He walked with uncertain steps over to the fire and sat down with his back to those still at the table.

"Oh dear," Norrie said in apology. "I'm terribly sorry. When he's upset, sometimes he speaks sternly."

"His lectures," Julia said, "they were so inspiring. I went to all of them with Paul." She met Norrie's eyes a moment, then broke the intense contact and looked down.

"Were you ever tempted," Kate asked Julia, "to take LSD yourself to help expand your spiritual experience?"

"No. Drugs and I somehow don't get along. I smoked marijuana a few times – but I prefer my inner world as it is, there's always something unexpected rising up."

She paused, looked to the kitchen and then surprised everybody by smiling slightly at an inward thought.

"I admit that sometimes," she went on, "I suddenly shift into deep spiritual feelings right in the middle of when I'm cooking. Isn't that strange? And right now I think I'll go check on the pie. More wine anyone? Paul was always saying, when he'd pour the first glass of his bottle: 'If it's good enough for Jesus, it's good enough for me.'"

20

The plan was simple. Ty laid it out to everyone except the Professor as they ate apple pie. There was, he explained, no telling if any person out there would bite. But as things currently stood evidence-wise, Jonathan was still the prime suspect even though everyone in Jon's cottage right now suspected the real murderer was still on the loose – so obviously something had to be done to flush that person into the open. It was a somewhat risky plan, but it was required.

Julia listened attentively, asked a few detail questions, then pushed her fears back and agreed to be the live bait in the plan, remaining alone in the house tonight, just in case somebody was watching the house and wanting to get at her when she was alone.

In Ty's strategy the Rosenblums would stay with her ten minutes after Kate and Ty drove off in their respective vehicles that were currently parked up in the lot. Then the Rosenblums would depart as well, leaving Julia all alone in the house at right around 10 pm. Aside from the Feds, anyone who'd read that note Ty had left on Rupert's door and wanted those films, or who wanted to find out if Julia knew where the LSD bottles were, might be tempted to approach the cottage – and bang, they'd get caught in Ty's trap just before they entered the house, because Ty and Kate would be hiding outside watching. Yes it was a long shot but it was the only shot Ty could think of.

One hitch to the plan that Ty pointed out was that Ty and Kate would have to drive off down the hill and then hike back up on the trail Ty had found – and Kate was not exactly attired for frolicking through the woods. She proved a good girl scout, however, always keeping a change of clothes in her car. And so as the evening came to an end, she and Ty said goodbye and off they walked up the path to the parking lot, as if departing for the night.

With the two police people suddenly gone and the front door closed, the house became almost deathly quiet. Bernie was still at the fire in a deep reverie and Julia returned to the kitchen. Norrie went over to the old man and spoke softly in his ear for a moment, then she stood upright, stared into the fire a long moment, then turned and walked into the kitchen to help wash the dishes.

Julia had her hands in hot water and looked tense. "Don't you worry," Norrie said softly to her, "those two out there will make sure nothing goes wrong."

"I don't really have the nerves for this sort of police thing," Julia admitted. "But here we are and it's happening and of course I'll do anything to help Jon."

"You've been to see him?"

"Kate said it was better if I didn't go down today."

"Jon is a wonderful young man. Some souls seem to have such inborn depth that sometimes I almost agree with the Hindus … we do perhaps come back, again and again. And, well – might I ask a question that's on my own mind, related to Bernie being so old and ready to depart – has, uhm, has Paul somehow returned to you, have you felt his presence beyond his physical, uhm, his physical demise?"

Julia just stared at her blankly. "What?"

"His spirit. Has it come to you, now that his mortal presence has departed?"

"Oh. Well. No. But we were never that close, heart to heart. I hungered for intimacy but he felt it was a human weakness. Paul, he sometimes seemed like a lost angel caught in a human body, a body that I loved but a mind that could drive the angel part of him crazy. Maybe we all have an angel part to us ... but I'm babbling – you were saying that you wonder if Bernie will come back to visit you somehow, after he dies?""

"Oh, it's him who talks about coming back after he goes. I most usually think that when we go, we're entirely gone. All this talk about Christians somehow ending up as eternal physical bodies – it just doesn't ring true deep inside. I've had a good life. I can let it go. Bernie should have been gone years ago, he's eleven years older than me so I forgive him his lapses, and I do pray he goes gently."

"I haven't prayed since I was little but I was praying this afternoon," Julia confessed. "I must ask – do you think God can really actually answer prayers, does he interfere in human events, make things happen one way or the other, influence the flow of life on this planet? I mean, with Paul getting shot in the head last night right over there in our cabin – really, where was God in that equation?"

"Oh, to be truthful, my own experience, quite contrary to Bernie's theology, is that God does not move mountains, he does not influence events or choose sides – except to the extent that people open up and let him into their hearts. Then yes, surely – at heart levels he can powerfully act through us mortals."

"For months, Norrie, it was so strange – in many ways Paul was already ... gone."

"Ahh. I feel somewhat the same with Bernie, and he worries me. Several times now outside any classroom, he's slipped into one of the prophets – and then he doesn't remember after. So, tell me now, dearie, how can I help, you know I love you, I want to support you through all this – are there plans yet for Paul's funeral?"

"His father phoned from New Jersey. The body is to be cremated and the ashes flown back east for a memorial service. I'm not going – Jon needs me here."

"You do love him."

"Yes."

"If you want to find God, I myself found that he's right there – alive in that spark that holds two people together. That's what humanity – oh, but look, it's past time for us to play our role in this little drama and I'm nervous for you, Julia. You must phone me later tonight, I'll be sitting up until you do."

Ten, fifteen minutes went by after the Rosenblums had departed and left Julia sitting alone on the sofa. The fire that Ty had built and re-stoked throughout the evening was now dying down, the flame almost gone. Julia got up and threw two oak logs on the embers, then bent over and blew hard several times. With the last blow the fire burst back into flame. She made herself think about Paul being cremated, she had to face facts and push through this numbness that was still insulating her.

She watched the flames turning the log into ashes and realized that at some level Paul was nothing more than ashes and dust now, his living presence entirely gone – and she wondered for the hundredth time that day why she still somehow felt that everything was exactly as it must be, that Paul for months had been fading out and now he was naturally gone – or rather very unnaturally gone.

And then out of the blue she got hit with the realization that had been hounding her – that if indeed Paul had somehow been some unique version of Jesus incarnate, then that terminal act of cremating his physical corpse, from a Christian point of view, would totally destroy any chance of his organic body rising physically up from the dead.

Standing up from the fire she felt dizzy, she had to reach out and put her hand quickly on the mantle over the fireplace to regain her balance. This is insane, she muttered to herself, staying here in this cottage alone like this tonight when just twenty-four hours ago some unknown maniac had been next door aiming and pulling the trigger of Jon's pistol and eradicating forever from the face of this earth, Paul's unique amazing personal consciousness

But then some voice inside her was saying, Julia, cut it out, relax. There's no way that Paul could become resurrected, walk this earth again, and then rise up to heaven – because there was no heaven up there at all. What utter idiocy to even imagine such an impossible fantasy.

She sat down on the sofa. Except for the fire popping and the fridge humming, the house was as quiet as a tomb. And there was no one, certainly no dreamy feminine Mary-duo, to watch as angels rolled some giant boulder away from the entrance to that tomb.

Her mind shifted, or expanded, somehow leapt to focusing on Jon sitting right at that moment down in his own tomb of a cell. Her heart was suddenly pounding loud in her ears, aching intensely inside her chest. She knew it had been wrong not to go see him – why had Kate insisted that she stay away from Jon all day? Who's side was that woman really on anyway? Jon was innocent and he needed loving companionship but he hadn't gotten any – at least not hers.

Her whole body felt shaky and weak but at the same time charged with some crazy emotion, she realized she was in danger of losing her emotional control and shrieking with panic, even though she kept reminding herself that there were two able police officers out there in the dark right now, hopefully poised in position. Julia's only job was to stay calm, stay low-key, and continue to be live bate inside Ty Hadley's killer trap.

She thought impulsively of putting on some music to help dispel the ghostly silence of the room. Padding in silent stocking feet, she went over to look through Jon's hefty album collection. Ah, there was Jesse Colin Young's first album ... 'come on people now, smile on your brother – everybody get together, try to love one another right now ...'

All Paul's grand talk the last few days of everyone loving one another, his perfect vision of universal peace and harmony – and then a bullet in his forehead and that's that, end of story. Just absolutely too stark. As she stood holding the album cover in her hands, hot tears welled – she felt suddenly the same helpless she'd felt that night back home when uncle Earl had stalked into her bedroom, grinning with his rotten whiskey breath, reaching out and touching her left breast – then reacting to her slap with his own slap.

Stop, don't think of that, she ordered herself. Think of Jon, or think of sanding a beautifully-grained piece of redwood or mahogany – think of being somewhere else, anywhere but here where murder and death and violence and cremation were all lurking everywhere, inside and outside, all around her in this goddamned darkness.

Outside a hundred yards down the steep overgrown hillside from Julia and the cottage, Ty was uncomfortable in the extreme but he didn't dare move a muscle. This whole plan hadn't been thought through properly, he and Kate should have worked out the details when they were still in the cabin. Was he now flubbing up his own son's murder case? Back home in cowboy Templeton things usually moved fast, he went hard and banged heads until the truth came out. Up here he was entirely out of his element, caught with zero idea which heads to bang.

He shifted his weight from one foot to the other in the darkness, keeping his eyes focused beyond the redwood trunk he was hiding behind, over to where the foot path up to the cottage was now all but lost in moon shadow. He was about halfway up the path from the lower road, having parked his car down at the singles dormitory lot, hiked fast the ten minutes on the back road to the path, then worked his way up through the underbrush on the right side of the path. It was a wide path and not too steep, anybody could park down on the road below and come up here in just a few minutes.

Kate by now should also be in position, up above the cottage. And Julie would be sitting alone inside sweating it out. He wasn't sure why he expected somebody to make a move on her or the cottage tonight – it was nothing more than a raw hunch but Kate had immediately gone along with the plan, she was a hunch cop too and that's what he liked about her, she knew how to ride with her hunches. Had that been some hunch of hers that'd made her come after him with those hungry hands grabbing him almost just like he was grabbing her? Loretta had been the opposite when he'd met her at Berkeley, she'd held back for months before letting him hardly touch her. Kate was right out of gate number five and he had to admit that she –

– his body tensed.

A slight snap was all he'd heard.

Now nothing. His breath was tight in his throat. If it was the CIA jerk, this was going to get nasty.

There it came again, closer down below. Footsteps, and now a dim pen light on the trail, coming up the path. Thirty feet away, twenty – a shadow figure in the dark walking quiet but fast up the trail under the black towering redwoods. Ty reached inside his Levi jacket and took out his .38, feeling suddenly goosed with energy as if he was back again caught in combat. He waited as long as he dared, then tensed to make his move – then pulled back just in time.

Someone else was coming up the path behind the first figure, somebody moving at the same speed but without a flashlight, and with a slightly different sound to his feet, what was that? Ah. Somebody with a limp. Decision time – if he jumped the second one right now, he'd most likely lose the first – and if Kate didn't act fast from the front, the first guy could get inside, shoot and run. Julia was in danger – but something held Ty back for three, four, five seconds after the second guy went by –

Then he went into action, dropped back onto the path and went running fast uphill through the darkness, random rays of moonlight showing him just enough of the trail so he didn't trip.

He rounded the bend in the path and saw the first figure going up the back steps to Jon's cottage. The second figure nearer to Ty hesitated, then moved on carefully so as not to be seen from above. The first figure paused outside the back door, then tried the door. It opened – why hadn't Julia locked the damn door! Ah, that was the door that had been banged in earlier in the day. Another error.

Ty instantly started running, knowing he was too far away to get both guys, only the closer one – but just as he made his move a third figure came running around from the side of the cottage shouting in a tough female voice:

"Police, freeze – raise your hands – now!"

Ty came up behind the second figure as it pivoted and started to run with a limp down the path. "Hold it right there."

"Don't – don't shoot," a tense male voice shouted back. "I mean, what the fuck!"

"Get up those stairs – now."

The two of them stomped loudly up the worn wooden steps, and then on into the house, following right on the heels of Kate and the man she'd apprehended. Julia was nowhere to be seen.

"Down on the couch, both of you," Kate ordered.

As they crashed down onto the sofa, the one without the limp muttered to the other one: "Damn you – just what the hell are you doing here?"

"I might ask the same of you," the other fired back. "What are you doing, breaking into Jon's – "

"Shut up. Just cool it!" the first guy growled.

Silence reigned, two cops towering over two captured intruders, two cop guns still out and threatening.

"So I wonder, who have we here?" Ty asked Kate, both of them catching their breaths.

"A couple of Jon's supposed friends," she said. "The one you caught is Douglas McFerrin, you met him at the police office. Mine is none other than Stuart Wilson."

"The sexy broad's husband?"

"And just who the fucking hell," Stuart demanded, "are you?"

Kate flashed her local shield.

He shrugged. "Idiots, running around with guns. I live just two doors down, I'm coming up the hill home, just stopping by to see how poor Julia's doing, and I get attacked. Police brutality – my lawyer's going to get right on your case."

Julia came walking out of the bedroom, right over to Stuart. "You were forcing your way in here without even knocking, you're the one who killed Paul!"

"Oh, now I get this," he said right back at her. "Obviously you don't believe Jon killed Paul – and hey, you're absolutely right. Finally my jealous wife, she told me what she really saw last night – the real killer."

"So – who was it?" Ty pushed him.

"Well here's what I know, and it's what I was coming here to tell Julia – right before Jonathan showed up at Paul's cabin, somebody came in and shot Paul, then ran out that back door when Jon came in the front. Then Julia here came in right after Jon. Whoever it was that Dana saw run off down the back porch, he's the one – she saw the killer escape."

"That's not what she told me," Ty said right back at him.

Stuart shrugged is shoulders, feeling fully in charge of the situation now. "Dana can be nasty when she's jealous – but hey, in the end she wouldn't have let the wrong guy hang."

"So then, why are you out sneaking around here tonight?" Kate demanded.

"I was just down at the single dorms looking for Reggie, and thought I'd stop by and tell Julia the good news – and this is what I get, copper abuse."

Stuart shifted slightly and Kate suddenly tensed. "Hold it," she growled. "Stand up, both of you, hands on your heads."

"Cut the shit," from Doug. "We're just students."

But Ty could see the bulge now. Talk about dumb, they hadn't searched them. "Stand up as ordered or you're down the hill for resisting arrest."

Stuart hesitated just a moment, then came to his feet, hands behind his head and a superior smirk on his face. "So frisk me but be cool, man, lay off the balls."

"You too, up," Ty said to Doug.

"Careful right there," Kate said to Ty.

She stood guard while Ty patted down Stuart. Clean except for a long-bladed pocket knife. But not so with Douglas McFerrin – snub-nose .38 in coat pocket.

"I'm legal, I have a license," he objected. He took out his wallet, flipped it open – took out a piece of paper, unfolded it and handed it to Kate. "I'm a Vet, my life was threatened a while ago so I carry a gun."

"Guns on a seminary campus?"

"Somebody shot Paul dead and it wasn't Jon. That means some maniac is still running around on the loose so yeah, I'm packing tonight, you bet."

"Explain to me right now why you were sneaking up behind this other guy with that gun?" Kate demanded.

Doug looked at Stuart. Ty couldn't see what passed between them. "I just happened to be coming up for the same reason. Julia has been through something terrible. I wanted to see how she was doing."

"There's always the phone," Ty said.

"Hardly personal enough, is it?"

"Depends on what you had in mind."

"Well, now you'll never know."

Soon thereafter Ty and Kate were marching the two men over two cottages to Stuart's place. Dana was standing by the side window looking out. The electric wall heater was glowing orange; the place was hot.

"I finally found you some police," Stuart told her.

"What's he doing here?" she said aggressively referring to Doug.

Stuart was impatient with her. "You need to give your statement to the cops so they can set Jon free."

"Dana," Ty spoke gruffly. "Earlier when I was here you didn't say you saw anyone come out that door."

"Sorry but I didn't tell any lies, I just didn't remember that detail. I was so frazzled I just – forgot."

"You'll need to come down to the station for a formal interview first thing in the morning," Kate informed her. "All three of you. But I want to hear right now, Dana – what exactly did you see last night?"

"Well first I heard them shouting, arguing, about fifteen minutes before the gunshot. Right after the shot I looked across to their house – and somebody came hurrying out the back door and then down the steps and off on that path into the night."

"Did you see the person well enough to identify them?" Ty asked urgently.

"Well – not really. It was too dark."

"Did you notice anything at all about the person?"

"Yes I did," she said. "But it's very uncomfortable to say it here. I don't mean to incriminate and it's not positive identification."

"What did you notice, Dana?"

"I'll tell you in private."

"Okay, out," Ty ordered the two guys.

"I have a meeting at eleven," Doug told him. "It's important, I've got to go."

"A meeting this late?" Ty asked.

Doug smiled his thin-lipped grin. "The Lord's work is never done. Am I being held for anything?"

"Just be at the station at eight tomorrow."

"Yes Ma'am."

He turned and walked with his slight limp out of the room. "Now what do you have to say?" Kate pressed.

"I want everybody out."

"Out," Ty said to Stuart.

"No, I want – "

"Out!" Kate shouted at him.

He considered reacting, but controlled himself – turned and walked in front of Ty outside the cottage.

Biting her lip, Dana faced the female cop. "So now, tell me," Kate asked her evenly.

"Alright. That person, whoever it was who took off running down those stairs over there, was going sort of slow, hobbling along with a limp or some such."

"You're sure of that?"

"I'm sure."

"Man or woman?"

"Hard to say."

"You'll swear to all this?"

"Why shouldn't I – it's the truth."

21

For months, long before Paul snapped into expanded consciousness, Reggie had become a regular participant in Steve Gorkin's Monday Night Class, downtown at San Francisco's Wonderland Theater. Along with around a thousand other college kids, Reggie just entirely dug the scene, listening with rapt attention to the teachings of this spiritual straight shooter. Steve was a young philosophy professor who'd taken psychedelics in a ritual with the poet Gary Snyder, or so Reggie'd heard, and just like Paul (except for the Jesus part) Steve seemed to have become a fully enlightened being.

With Paul so suddenly and violently dead, Reggie decided to get himself across the bridge to receive a good solid hit of Gorkin's out-flowing compassion and wisdom. After Douglas and Stuart ignobly dumped him at his dorm that afternoon, he proved he could navigate while flying super-high by aiming his old Ford Fairlane down south toward the City. He was early, so he got some tacos at a local stand, took a walk in the dusky evening, then headed for the giant full-circle indoor performance center.

The crowd at the Wonderland was on fire when he got there because Jorma Kaukonen and Jack Cassidy of the Jefferson Airplane were on stage, playing an electric-guitar and bass raga duo that steadily built faster and faster into a frenzy, then seemed to burst into musical infinity and then calm down afterwards like they'd had some kind of mutual musical orgasm that faded into silent perfection.

Right after that, the humble yet great Steve Gorkin took the stage. Bearded and calmly charismatic, he stood there alone in the spotlight with a mike in his hand for a long moment, not saying anything at all – then as usual on Monday nights, when he felt good and ready he started talking – not with the commanding voice of Jesus incarnate like Paul had tuned onto, but as far as Reggie was concerned, allowing a similar truth of Spirit to enter and talk through him. It was definitely almost like Spirit had talked through Paul, and Reggie soaked it up like a hungry sponge, needing to hear again and again about the infinite force of forgiveness, the invincible power of turning the other cheek, the eternal wisdom of detaching from all fear-based low-brain emotions and rising up through the seven chakras, one by one, everyone together in the audience following Gorkin's voice into the ethereal higher realms. Probably 99 percent of the people in the auditorium were high on something or other, it was a remarkable group experience like always ...

Reggie felt his breathing step by step get the message, relax and soften. He leaned back in his seat, feeling confident the Movement was still intact even if Paul was gone. As Gorkin talked on and on in his strong low voice, Reggie found himself accepting that whoever had shot Paul and for whatever reason, it was all still all in the flow, Spirit was still in charge, chaos was not loose upon the world. Life, death, life again – it was all so much more vast than the thinking mind could even begin to imagine.

Gorkin fell silent, lowered the mike. The spotlight moved and found two young women sitting on round pillows. One of the women started playing her Japanese shakuhachi flute very softly but amplified in the great high-ceilinged hall so the vast volume of air seemed to become alive with resonant vibration.

"Words, even like what I'm saying to you now," Steve was saying to his audience, his voice seeming to merge seamlessly with the flute, "are not the vehicle for deep experience but they point your attention, that's the power of words – to help you aim your attention directly toward the inner source of experience, of knowing, of God. All you do is quiet your mind, breathe into this eternal moment, and start to listen to your own inner muse who is always there, always waiting to talk to you and through you. Right now choose to stop being a cognitive manipulator. Become a full participant in this greater whole. Brush aside the unconscious stuff erupting out of your ego mind. Focus fully on the whole … pop inside right here right now."

He fell silent, turned and walked to the back of the stage, out of the limelight as the meditative flute music continued. Reggie wished he had a joint but nobody near him seemed to be lighting up and hell, it didn't matter, he was already high and the music was taking him and everybody in the auditorium even higher.

Gorkin started talking again. "Alan across the bay, he and I were talking a couple days ago about all this leadership thing. Alan sees Spirit guiding each of us individually without the need of a leader to point the way and sure, I've been there, done that. But there is also the essential dynamic of brother helping brother."

He paused and looked out over these thousand human beings he was consciously sharing space with. He continued looking, taking them in. "I doubt if any of you would be here tonight if you weren't seeking spiritual guidance. So I'm willing to get up and let Spirit act through me. But you also are the leader – there's nothing between you and life, you and God, you and me right now."

He paused and said nothing for five breaths, then ten. Then he was moved to speak again. "Look constantly to your own breathing, that's where you come from, where you go to. Stop breathing altogether and soon you feel the life force saying hey – time for an inhale. That's God talking from the epicenter of the eternal breath pulsation. No past and equally no future. Your heart going kabooah kabooah – feel life ... breathing you."

Silence filled the auditorium. The hush itself seemed almost alive. Reggie felt himself floating, at home in his heart ... and his heart at home in some greater heart. "There's nothing to do right now," Steve was saying softly, "so stop making any effort at all. Come to a total absolute standstill. Surrender your heart and soul to merge into infinite peace. Observe clearly that you are not making yourself breathe. Some higher being is right now and always breathing with you and through you – and that higher being has a voice. That voice is speaking through me right now. Hello, I am. Love. Dig it."

Someone shouted from way in back behind Reggie but it was muffled. Steve cocked his ear a moment, heard no more, went on. "You breathe, you love, you pass away, that's life on this planet. A guy I met this weekend up in San Anselmo, Paul Jacobs, maybe some of you heard him talking – he stopped breathing last night. I just got word. Somebody went up and shot this totally beautiful guy – dead. Bang. Imagine that – suddenly going from being radically alive and totally

plugged into that voice like Paul was, then here comes
somebody into your house and bang – you're dead."

He shook his head of scraggly long hair. "We
cannot dodge our own fate. When it's time, it's time.
Give me one moment of orgasm and I'll trade it for ten
years of bored suburban subsistence. Our time will
come."

Somebody shouted something to him, he paused
and listened. Reggie couldn't hear what was being said
but Gorkin stood and listened attentively as he often did.
"Well," he said finally in response to the question, "I
don't know if he was enlightened. Am I – are you? I don't
have those answers. Maybe that whole enlightenment
thing is just an idea, a head-trip, a thought to let go of.
Just pay attention to the air flowing in and out of your
nose right now, totally feel it. Also feel the movements in
your chest and belly as you breathe – look right there,
that's you. Go ahead and tune into whatever feelings you
find inside, right in the center of your heart – there's
God, right there. It doesn't take acid, it doesn't take ten
years at the ashram. Just do it. Right now. The air flowing
in. Flowing out. Through us all. Life. Death. Life. All
together now ..."

Some time later, about midnight, Reggie came walking
outside with the big hushed crowd of people, feeling for
the first time since Paul had been killed like the world
could continue without Paul's presence. He looked
around the parking lot for somebody he might know;
usually he'd spy a few friends from across the bay but
tonight no such luck, even though he was aching for
some regular people to hang out with a bit, smoke one
down, get loose.

"Reggie, there you are."

He spun around and spied Doug from the Seminary standing right behind him. "Hey, what's happening?"

"I was looking for you," Doug said. "I figured you'd come here, your usual Monday habit. Hey, I have good news. Come hop in, let's talk – there are things to do tonight."

Not feeling certain at all, Reggie went with Doug over to a spanking-new Volkswagen camper. They got in the side door and sat there together in the metal cocoon. Douglas was eyeing him strangely in the close dark quarters and Reggie felt slightly uncomfortable. "So what's up?" he asked. "Hey, you gotta joint?"

"No, no – but, just between you and me?" Doug confided in a low confident voice.

"Sure, zip lip."

"Well I went and broke into Jon's car just now, up at the Seminary lot. And guess what I found in the trunk?"

"Hey – four bottles of acid!"

"Close. I found a piece of paper tucked away. Took me ten minutes to find it, had to hide twice when people came driving into the lot. Cryptic note but I knew what he was describing – this is just between you and me, you clear on that? We need to play this very cool. I want you to go and get in your car like we're going our separate ways. There's Narcs in this audience, believe me. So just drive off heading home but then circle over to the Park, on the north side. Park on Fulton close to the North Windmill – you know where that windmill is, we were there with Jon and Paul and Julia a while back, that Sunday of the concert, remember?"

"Sure I remember. But – "

"So that's where he seems to have hid the bottles. The paper gives the pacing details we'll follow. So see you there – I'm counting on you, don't get lost."

Reggie was excited now, he jumped out of the VW and got into his old machine, feeling good. Douglas was finally treating him like an equal. Fuck, four quarts of Sandoz in hand tonight – use like a cup to blow Sacramento, sell the rest and be a rich man just like that, it was all happening. Maybe Paul was gone but the flow continues, like Gorkin said – no one can stop Spirit from busting loose.

He took a wrong turn and ended up down on Ashbury and he lost ten minutes before he got to the Park and was walking through all the gardens and the lawns. This was a dark part of the Park and things weren't as cool hang-wise here as last year, there was way too much hard stuff going around. Over to his left in the moonlight, he could now see the big circular windmill that some crazy Dutch guy had donated money to build way back when. It was still working, keeping water flowing down the little stream and all. Kind'a romantic – but a strange place to stash the quarts, they must be buried over in the shrubs somewhere.

"Hey!"

Reggie turned at the sudden voice coming from the side of the windmill. "I got lost," he admitted, walking over.

"Come around back here where we won't be seen," Doug told him quietly.

As Reggie followed Doug behind the granite edifice he realized that the usually straight-looking Air Force guy had put on a bit of disguise, red bandana headband and no leather jacket – some slouch jacket instead, zipped up.

"Hey, you look good like that," Reggie said. "Anyway where's the stuff, Jon must have dug a hole."

Doug was casually gripping a pistol in his left hand. "Hey," Reggie reacted, "put that thing away, cops all over here, they'll snap you, holding heat right out in the open."

"Relax, I checked just now," Doug told him, "there's nobody around except a few druggies."

"Well put it away anyway." Reggie looked down again at the pistol in Doug's right hand. "I mean, that's a .22 just like what killed Paul."

Doug grinned the strangest grin. Light suddenly dawned.

"No, you're not the one who – what – don't tell me you, I mean, like, you shot Paul?"

"Well in all honesty," Doug confided, "that's the most difficult issue – no, I didn't shoot Paul. Furthermore I don't know who did. Do you?"

"Hey, no idea but come on, like, put that thing away. Please Doug – I mean it, that's not funny."

22

Ty popped up from sleep. There was a breeze slipping in through the half-open window chilling his exposed left knee. She was there in bed beside him. Light was trying to push through the blackness outside. He pulled the covers up, made sure she was snug – thought fleetingly about Dana's shaky evidence and his son's imminent release – then fell asleep again feeling somehow that, all things considered, the universe must still be unfolding pretty much as it should.

Two hours later it was her turn to surface, the ringing of her phone waking her up. Reaching for it, she was hit with the blatant fact that there was a big tough lovely cowboy in bed with her.

"What?" she muttered into the phone.

"I need you down here right now," Sergeant Walkins blurted out.

"Oh no, what now?"

He told her. She hung up and got out of bed fast. Ty was watching her, looking at her nakedness and grinning that delicious grin of his.

"Forget that," she grumbled at him, "get saddled, we're off again."

She went into the bathroom but left the door open. "I'm starving," he shouted after her.

"Later."

"What happened?"

"Another shooting."

He sat up, trying to get his head around that. "But – where's Julia?" he blurted.

"Downstairs, you don't remember?"

"All I remember is you – but yeah, I remember now."

"Come in here, Ty, let's shower – save time."

She was definitely dead. From a gunshot wound to the head. Kate and Ty stood looking down at her a long moment, side by side with Officer Walkins.

"How many shots fired from the pistol?" Kate asked.

"Two. One through the ceiling there, and one through her head."

Kate nodded, stared at the dead woman's body another long moment, then silently stepped back and walked out with Ty so that the county forensics team could go to work on the room.

In the parlor they found the devastated lover sitting slouched down on a sofa that sported a beautiful view out through half-pulled curtains into the back yard where delicate rays of sunlight were just beginning to touch here and there with the glory of a new day that Stella didn't perceive one iota.

Kate closed the door, sat in a chair across from the young woman. Ty remained standing, holding his hat.

"We need to talk just a bit," Kate said softly to her.

For a moment she didn't seem to notice the words. Then she slowly turned her head from where she was staring outside into nothingness. "I'm guilty, I could have stayed and stopped her," she said, her voice a coarse constriction, "but – she told me to leave! She fired over my head and I ran, what else could I do, she was out of her mind."

"Had she been violent with you before?"

"What? Violent? Oh no, never. Only when I deserved punishment of course. But she was fair. She was harsh in the Lord but she was fair."

"You phoned from the Travelodge Motel down the road two miles from here."

"I should have gone right to the police with her in that condition, but she would have killed me – I mean she would have never forgiven me if I did such a thing. But now – this. She was such a beautiful being, she wouldn't do this to herself – someone came in and killed her."

"Was someone threatening her?"

"Oh always there were people angry at her – she did have a way of challenging the disbeliever. But no, no one would ever do this."

"Night before last, Sunday night, she went to the meeting at the Administration Building across campus. Did you go with her?"

"Oh no, I don't go with her ever, I am in charge of the house here."

"Did she drive?"

"Wilma always walked to the Seminary unless it was raining, she believed that her hip would heal if she exercised it enough, so that night like always, yes, she walked."

"Did she get a ride back home?"

"I told you, she walked."

"Do you remember her entering the house?"

"Yes, and she was distraught, the entire circumstances of the boy becoming Jesus had driven her to distraction. It's because of him, all this, it's all his fault."

"At what time did she get home on Sunday night?"

"I didn't look at a clock."

Sergeant Walkins was at the door. "Excuse me but Kate, we need you in here – right now."

Kate and Ty followed his big bulk down the hallway into the room. He pointed their attention to a note pad over on the big desk. "It was turned over," he said. "Otherwise I would have seen it earlier."

Ty looked over Kate's shoulder and they read the sprawling handwriting on lined yellow paper:

I am guilt in my heart, but someone must stop them – do not destroy, do not burn his body! Crucify me, take me! Satan was always hidden here inside me, all these years no one guessed – and now I'm lost and

Kate looked up into Ty's eyes. He shrugged his shoulders. Her face seemed totally drained, she looked like some forever-suffering being overwhelmed by the inherent unstoppable insanity of the human species. She glanced across the room, over to her left. Almost out of eyeshot was Dr. Franklin, the county med, looking very poorly himself, staring out at that same manicured back yard that God's neutral light was now brightening even further.

Kate walked over and sat near him in a straight-back chair. He raised his eyes and looked to her. "Wilma was my minister, all these years," he said.

"I'm so sorry."

"I know you are, Katie, and thanks for that."

"But I need to know."

"What – yes. Single small-caliber gunshot wound to the left temple, .22, almost certainly self-inflicted."

"How certain?"

"Unless somebody was standing right there with the muzzle pressed against her head, she did it herself – but why? You tell me that, Katie, you tell me that!"

"Calm down, please. Did you see the note?"

"Sorry. Yes I did, just now when Walkins found it. But Satan in her? No! That woman was on fire with the Lord, Kate. On fire with the Lord."

"What about her friend Stella?"

"Couldn't hurt a fly."

"You're sure?"

"Right now I'm not sure of anything at all – Wilma could be a harsh person but she was a good person. She must have been in utter spiritual despair to take her own life. And the alcohol – she'd been drinking last night, a great deal even though alcohol was a vice she preached against with venom. There's the Devil at play here, you mark my words."

"Maybe you give Stella a sedative, take her upstairs."

"Katie, you listen to me, you're an innocent in a quagmire here, this was the Devil's hand at work, you've got to get yourself out and away from all this type of evil happening, quit your job – it's poison to someone as pure as you. It's no life at all, following evil around the town. First that boy, now her. Who's next?"

23

It was nine o'clock before they made it down to the station. Dana was there impatiently waiting for them. And as they'd promised, both of the men from last night were there as well. Ty had half-expected them not to be present and was set to go hunt them down. Now he wasn't quite sure what to do with his time.

"I'll go get coffee and donuts," he offered.

"Already on their way. The interviewing will take an hour, then it'll be another hour before we get your Jonathan out. What about you go and talk with people on the list, that is if you're still interested in solving this case."

He headed out of the building. The cab of his pickup was chilly with damp cold air and the heater didn't blow hot until he was through the Seminary gate (no guard on duty today, he noted) and parked in front of the Administration Office. He sat in the cab a long moment, relatively low on momentum for continuing with the case now that Jon was seemingly in the clear. But that girl Dana's evidence was shaky, he knew that. He also knew that on general principle he'd stick around here until the murderer was found – he couldn't just up and leave when there could be more violence, especially with Jon and Julia still living here. Somebody shoots somebody, that shooter's got to go down.

The President of the Seminary wasn't in yet, but Ty struck a bit of gold at the first of the three houses he knocked at, on the back street just down the trail from Jon and Paul's cottages. A solitary widow answered the door. She was elderly but sharp, bent over about double from some spine problem but feisty as could be, the kind of old woman Ty enjoyed bantering with. She let him right in, not afraid of strangers – hey, at that age, what was there to be afraid of really, except fear itself like Roosevelt used to say.

Her kitchen was hot and cozy and her coffee strong. Ty was starving and her intuition grabbed on that fact, frying him three eggs and bacon and loving the intrusion into her solitary day.

"You have a good view from that window," he noted.

"Oh yes, I know most of what goes on around my own house, to be sure," she informed him. "That's my television right there, that window but the bulb went out on the street light, I phoned for the city to get it fixed. All sorts of kids doing all sorts of things right in their cars down there, and up that trail too. The youth these days, even the Christian youth, my goodness."

"Sunday night, day before yesterday – do you remember that specific day?"

"There's only one way to keep hold of your marbles and that's to play with them," she told him. "One of my games is watching who comes around and seeing what they do. I know most of the seminary kids by sight but not by name of course, I don't make it outside much anymore. Ever since Harvey died people from the church bring in my food and take me where I need to go, which isn't much since he's been gone, bless his soul. But day before yesterday was the shooting, of course I heard it, I'm never asleep before midnight. It's so quiet here and it's just a leap and a jump up to those cabins through the trees, the sound passes right through and I'm listening to all sorts of goings on up there, in the evenings especially. So certainly I heard that discharge of a weapon, it wasn't loud, just a sudden sharp crack in the night."

Ty finished off his coffee and she was up on her ancient feet pouring him some more. "So where was I, what was I saying?" she asked, losing her train of thought.

"Sunday night. The gunshot."

"Yes, well. Comings and goings. Like I said, I don't know names. And I admit that I was in my bathroom when I heard the shot. What I can tell you is that maybe ten minutes before the shot when I was still here sitting at the table, there was a car that pulled up and parked down by the path entrance there. I didn't pay it any special mind, kids park there, do their sex things, you must know that."

"Do you remember what kind of car?"

"Surely I do, parked right under that light and all, I could see it was blue, a soft blue, one of the older Chevrolet Bel Airs with the big fins on them, I remember because Harvey, he bought us one of them in '56 when it was brand new. That was how he went out, you know, he was a fast driver and the cancer was just eating him up by then and the pain was something terrible. So he up and went of for a drive and just ran his brand new Chevy off down into the ocean they told me, over by Bolinas. He used to take me driving over to Bolinas on a Saturday and then, after the Seminary put him out to pasture, any day I wanted."

"Did you see anyone get out of the car?"

"No, I'm right sorry but that's when Mother Nature came a'calling and I went into the bathroom, you know some things can't wait and I count my blessings that the call still comes regular, that I do. Truth is, modesty aside, I was sitting down doing my duty when I heard the shot. By the time I was up and around again, that car was gone."

24

Ty found the houseboat of Alan Watts much to his liking, a bit rustic and thoroughly comfortable, the whole edifice rocking just slightly upon a beautiful little blue inlet of the bay. He was also surprised to find that the scrawny Englishman on board was likewise at least somewhat to his liking.

They were relaxing alone together outside on the houseboat's upper deck in comfortable old canvas chairs sharing a whiskey. "I've read a few of your books recently," Ty told him, "just to keep up on what my son's into. He thinks the world of you, or so he says."

"Yes, and me him as well," Alan agreed, leaning back in his chair.

"You seem to live a bit out on the edge of society here, no judgment intended – I do the same in my own rancher way."

"My natural proclivity seems to be on the edge, always has been. Drove my Mum to distraction."

"I can imagine. To be honest, I'm not a great sympathizer of this whole psychedelic situation, I wasn't pleased when Jon got involved with that research outfit back at Princeton. But all the Zen part of your writings, that stuff attracted me, I've got a similar way of looking at things. Reality's reality. No one fights it and wins, my own papa liked to say that when we struggled against the flow of things – weather and disease and so forth. I like how you advise people to stay heads up, shush the internal chatter and focus on what's actually happening, otherwise you're going to get hurt – basic horse sense."

"'Yes, on all fronts. I'm honored that you've read so deeply into my writings."

"There's not much else to do back home come night time, I've always had a proclivity, as you might say, for philosophical reading. Me and my wife shared that and I continue now she's gone. Jonathan picked it up early but he was mostly reading science fiction and big fat biology books."

"I must admit, Mister Hadley, you appear more contemporary than I'd expect for a rancher. Jon told me you went to Berkeley for a short time."

"Until the War pulled me out – obviously not the Vietnam war, of which I'm not a fan. My kid brother Chris was over there fighting – not at all parallel to the war in Europe. When I came home my dad needed help on the ranch and then kids came and Dad got killed – otherwise I'd have gone back to school and got deeper into all those sharp German thinkers. Funny how I ended up killing a bunch of them."

"Must be frustrating, living way out in nowhere unplugged from the buzz of this new culture."

"Every day I'm out in nature doing physical work I love, then most evenings I'm snug in my easy chair reading up a storm. You're my age, around fifty?"

"A bit over."

"You wrote about taking LSD. I was wondering if you came up with that 200% notion of reality out of the blue, or did that come from taking drugs?"

"That was long before LSD, over in Japan. One morning in meditation it became crystal clear to me that two equal and opposite perspectives can co-exist perfectly in my mind, there's always opposites interacting in the universe. Why not let go of thinking either-or, and think inclusively – get beyond the dilemma of paradox."

"Yep – again, just common horse sense."

They fell silent a moment, gazing out over the rippling surface of the little inlet. "So do you have an interest in taking LSD?"

"No sir," Ty reacted. "I'll find what I'm looking for without drugs – they knock your horse sense all to hell and gone."

"There are millions of young people right now crying out for liberation from the mental prisons imposed upon them from birth onward by the holy priests, the school teachers, the confused parents, the meddling government. Psychedelics and cannabis can deliver a giant boost for initiating that leap into a totally-new freedom of the mind, they're a spiritual exploration tool of great value."

"I still don't like my son taking them."

"Jon is going to be one of America's true bright lights in consciousness research. From his experiences at the Institute, he knows from the inside-out that we are all a billion times more than we think we are. Science is right on the edge of a radical unexplored frontier – and Jon will be leading the way."

"He came home last summer half out of his wits, struggling to reclaim his own soul, he could hardly sit a horse for days. And get this – last week some CIA guys came by claiming Jon stole four quarts of LSD from that Institute."

"Yes, they were here recently as well. Let me tell you in full privacy a key reality orient to all this – the man currently running the CIA, Alan Dulles, was once the head of our OSS in Bern and even way back then, our military was interested in chemicals that could blow people's minds. The CIA's been working with psychedelics for over ten years now and yes, the Institute was part of that LSD research push, funded by the CIA through NIH."

"And Jon says you were part of all that."

"Did he? Well we mostly held our independent center. Then last year, along with Dick and Ralph, I pulled out of that entire mess – and made damn sure I pulled your boy out with me."

"Well thanks for that – but the LSD they say Jon stole, do you know where those bottles are right now?"

"No," Alan said honestly, "Jon won't tell me. I went by yesterday at the jail and talked with him."

"You must realize that Jon's just off the ranch and totally over his head in all this. I'm here to find who murdered his friend and I begin to suspect that those four missing bottles and the seminary murder might be associated. I understand that four quarts of pure LSD is enough to damage the minds of millions of our youth?"

"Stop that line of thinking, it's CIA-infested through and through. My own observation is that for every bad experience on LSD there will be ten, fifty, a hundred long-term enlightening experiences."

"According to the New Yorker the jury's still out on that," Ty said right back at him. "Meanwhile we've got a murderer somehow related to those potent quarts still running loose. You talk about tapping intuitive hunches in your books – you know the situation around here pretty good. What's your intuition telling you about that Paul boy's murderer?"

"I've been asking myself that same question but my intuition has come up with nothing – in fact, to go esoteric on you for a moment, there's a very strange psychic haze hovering over that murder."

"Are you saying that you have no faces, names, hunches for me to look into?"

"Just – no. Well – maybe. There's this one person in Jon's seminary circle that strikes me really just slightly wrong. I don't mean to incriminate, but you might want to check out Doug McFerrin. Older guy, 'Nam vet, hangs out with Jon and those other two, Stuart and Reggie. He's hard as rocks – I suspect he's up to something, I can't say what but somehow I've just never liked nor trusted him."

25

Jon meanwhile in his solitary situation had heard almost nothing of what was happening beyond his stuffy basement cell. But breakfast had again been quite thankfully good, a genuine three-egg ham-and-Ortega cheese omelet and hash-browns that temporarily in and of itself made him feel like life was worth living – even though the grumpy policeman who brought it down to him had said nary a word about his case.

Therefore the sudden appearance of the woman cop and the quick unlocking of his cell and the smile with which she greeted him felt like a wave of pure white magic sweeping through the dungeon.

"Jon, I'm very happy to tell you that you're as of this moment free to go," she said, and stepped right up and gave him a warm human hug, just like that.

"What – you caught the killer?" he asked eagerly.

"Not exactly but somebody in an adjoining cottage saw someone other than you come out the back door of Paul's cabin just after the gunshot. That evidence overrides you being found inside later with the pistol. And there was a suicide just now, the minister of the church. She might have been involved. Enough evidence to free you but you're not entirely off the hook by any means."

"Good enough for me."

"Some friends are waiting upstairs to give you a ride back to campus. Your father Tyson is off interviewing people, he'll meet us at my house up the hill around noon. Here's my address and phone, please be there. Julia's waiting for you now at your cottage – bring her too. Forgive me, I need to run."

At the top of the stairs, standing around eagerly awaiting his imminent appearance, were Stuart and Douglas, and there was also Dana off to the side caught up in some inner huff. Right then Jon wanted to be alone with Julia and his Dad, not these three – but there they were and a ride was a ride.

"Hey, thanks for coming," he said to the threesome. They hugged and then walked quickly together out of the police station into the coolness of the January morning.

"Your incarceration," Stuart intoned, "was a perfect example of the entire rank unfairness of the American judicial system, I tell you we're right on the verge of a police state is what we are – how're you feeling?"

"Like I could fly down these steps – ah, the air smells so good!"

"So how bad did they work you over?"

"Not at all, the woman cop seemed actually mostly on my side."

"So they didn't force any info out of you?"

"Like what?"

"Like the quarts."

"How would they know anything about that?"

"When they start pulling out finger nails, you start spilling things they didn't even know to ask."

"Get serious, Stu. This isn't Vietnam, this is sunny California."

"Well I'm glad you're out," Dana said, finally speaking up on his other side, with Doug walking with his limp on ahead to the old classy car.

"So tell me," Jon said to her, "was it you who saw the guy going out of Paul's cottage?"

"Yeah, so what?"

"So thanks."

"But I really did see somebody!"

"I wasn't saying you didn't."

They piled into the old Plymouth, Doug at the wheel, Dana up front as per Stu's insistence, and Stu getting in back with Jon.

"Where to?" Doug asked.

"Up to my place," Jon told him. "Right now I want to find Julia."

And so off they went. Stu let a few breaths go by in silence, then got to the work at hand. "Thing is, Jon, a lot's happened while you were in there. We're all set for action."

"I've had about all the action I want."

"But it's not like the revolution stopped after Paul got killed – in fact it's heating up right now, around all of that. People are set to become outraged over the assassination and the time has come for your Sandoz to get put on the table and stirred into the equation, just like we were talking."

"Like you were talking, not me, remember?"

"Come on, Jon. Have a heart. I've worked hard and just yesterday we lined up the perfect distributor over in Oakland, it's all set to roll out. We'll clear a dollar a hit, then everybody does what they want. For me, all my earnings flow into the movement, every penny. And you?"

"No, Stu. Just no."

"But I've promised to bring the jars over tomorrow morning, they'll have the cash, it'll get out to millions at less than half price, that's the agreement – it'll be that final psychic push that wakes up the country's sleeping tiger."

"No is no. I'm going to just settle back a while. I mean, Paul's barely in the ground and you're acting like life is back to normal. Give me a break. So where's his body, what's happening on that front?"

"Who the fuck cares about where somebody's body is," Stuart retorted, "Paul's spirit is now long gone from his physical body. Hey slow down," he said to Doug, looking out the side window, "what's going on over there?"

They drove past several parked police cars and a bunch of local gawkers.

"Doug, isn't that the minister's house?"

"Uhm, I'm not sure," Doug lied casually as he drove past.

"Look, all I'm asking," Stuart continued with Jon, "is for you to do your natural part for the Movement, give me a quick map or something, do what's right for the higher good."

"Well let me decide the higher good on this."

"But something's got to set the fire and you're holding the fuse, you know that. The Brotherhood distributor, Reggie's friend, he says he'll sell for way below half price so that everybody can afford to get off this coming weekend – that's the blow-date at Berkeley with the Weathermen, we just found out, we're coordinating with them, Reggie helped to set all that up yesterday, they're expecting us to come through. And media-wise we've got super hot reporters set to cook. I'm telling you Jonathan – it's happening."

"So – enough of all that. I just want to find Julia," Jon told him bluntly, his patience wearing thin, "and then I need to touch base with my dad – and not deal with anything else right now, got me?"

"No, I don't get you – this is serious. You're either with us or against and if you're against, that's not good."

"Are you actually somehow threatening me here, is that what's happening?"

"I'm just talking reality," Stuart said right back. "Plans have been made, deals agreed to. You need to go get the bottles – then you're free to do what you want."

"So where's Reggie?"

"I don't know. Doug, you seen Reggie?"

"Reggie? No, not since we dropped him off last night at his dorm, around dinner time."

"So what say?" Stu pressed Jon. "Paul's down – we owe it to him to carry on the good work."

"Well who shot Paul? You tell me."

"I have zero idea."

"I'll bet," Jon grumbled.

"Now what' that shit," Stu reacted.

"Maybe somebody from New York days did it," Jon told him, "and you're the one who knows his past."

"Well maybe somebody did come in from the old times, Paul wasn't always Jesus, he played heavy and left."

"Maybe they'll come after you too," Jon said.

"No way."

"How come?"

"I was the original clean machine. But I'm telling you, Reggie's Oakland gang will come over here looking for you if we don't come through with the acid. Spirit inspired you to grab that acid – now you've got to play along."

"Fuck you. Douglas, stop the car," Jon ordered, totally fed up.

They were two blocks away from the Seminary entrance. Stuart nodded and Douglas pulled over. Jon opened his door. "Enough of this," he growled. "I'm a free man, I do what feels right, not what you tell me."

Julia'd had enough waiting. Kate had again asked her not to come to the station. Julia still trusted her – but her patience was gone. She had a suitcase packed, she was moving out of the whole Seminary scene, headed up to the spare bedroom Kate had offered her. Jon could stay there too if he chose to – all that mattered to Julia right then was being gone from this deathly locale forever.

But just as she was set to walk out of her cottage the phone rang. She hesitated, then picked it up.

"Ah, thank you for answering," Kate said over the line, her voice tense. "Listen carefully – Jon is on his way to your cottage. Both of you must drive up to my house, stay there until we get back. Don't tell anyone where you're going. There's been another shooting."

"On no!"

"Ty and I'll be back to the house as soon as we can. Use the hot tub out on the back balcony, relax, make some lunch – we'll have a celebration tonight."

Kate hung up and Julia walked fast out the door, heading up the path with her suitcase to meet Jon in the parking lot. Just when she got to the lot a shiny old sedan that she recognized as Stuart's came roaring up the hill over-fast and slid to an abrupt halt just a few feet away from her. The driver's door opened and Douglas McFerrin got out and headed fast toward her.

Two other doors opened at the same time as both Stuart and Dana jumped out and came running after Doug, shouting at him. "Doug, stop, not here," Stuart ordered him from behind. "You're acting crazy, listen to me!"

But Doug didn't stop nor did he listen. Julia, tensing in fear, started fast toward Jon's car – but Doug overtook her, grabbed her arm and pulled her to a stop.

"Julia, just relax now and come with us a bit, we have things to talk over," he told her in a low grumble.

Julia tried to break free but he was gripping her hard and she cried out in pain. Dana came rushing up and grabbed Doug. "You fucking bully, you leave her alone," she shouted at him, sounding almost hysterical and making a scene.

His reaction was a fast swing of his free hand that slapped Dana hard in the face and knocked her away – and then Stuart was suddenly there, swinging a fist and hitting Doug right smack hard in the face.

With his nose spurting blood and the pain intense, Doug let go of Julia and turned fast and furious to accost Stuart, both of them breathing hard. "Now you shouldn't have done that," he muttered.

"Snap out of it, Doug," Stuart ordered, "look, there's people over there watching, get right back in the car before you fuck up everything."

Doug turned his head – two Seminary couples had in fact just come walking up from the cottages and were stopped fifty feet away, watching the violent situation anxiously.

"Fuck," Doug mumbled, his back to Julia – who took the opportunity to grab her suitcase and hurry away and get to Jonathan's car. Without waiting to see what would happen between the two men, she jumped into the driver's seat, jammed the key in the ignition, and drove fast down Holy Hill.

As she turned onto Ross Avenue, her mind a blank, she almost ran into some guy walking up the street. She screeched to a stop, jumped out and went running back up the road – and right into Jon's arms.

26

Liquid balm. Steamy calm. Bodies utterly at rest, tingling with the hot tub's watery massage and post-coitus flush of lingering hormones. Jon had come with such emotion and explosion that he was now just effortlessly drifting in the hot tub across from her, feeling as if not only his body but his whole being was languidly aloft and weightless. The second glass of white wine was half gone and loosening the mental muscles even more as he slowly realized that yes, it was over, he was out of jail and she was here safe with him.

The drive up the curvy road to Kate's house with Julia at the wheel had been crazy, both of them talking at the same time and him reaching and grabbing and squeezing her leg with obvious carnal intent, then burrowing his nose into her soft scented hair and neck, recklessly distracting her from her driving – then both of them half-running into the big old house and her leading him by the hand fast into the downstairs back bedroom where she was as furious as he was to get out of clothes and get him all the way inside her.

Now she stretched like a satisfied cat and reached for her wine, breasts in the process rising above the water, same nipples he'd gobbled just fifteen minutes earlier while consumed in a passion he'd never quite known before. He gazed at her natural animal beauty, the nipples slightly up-tilted, breasts just right, just absolutely almost unbearably perfect, all over.

He floated over to her as she was sipping her wine and she smiled that languid slack-lip smile of hers that had caught his breath the very first time he'd met her. But those same lips now seemed to tremble just slightly, as if some inner earthquake was in progress. He brought her gently against him and as she commenced crying he held her a very long time because there was a very great big cry inside her that couldn't remain inside a moment longer without perhaps doing her psyche permanent damage of some kind.

And then at some point, through the miracle precision of God's sexual plumbing, once again he was inside her and all sorts of subterranean passions merged into one flow by a wholebody kiss that threatened to become endless, turning the tub water into a turbulent splashy sea as their bodies comingled yet again.

Meanwhile there were other minds fixating sharply on them. But it all seemed far too simple – of course the lady cop would provide safe haven and offer her place but Stuart already knew the cop's name and the name was in the phone book and the address was right there too. What fools these mortals be, he thought to himself. Especially these local cop fools who never had to face anything bigger than a parking violation.

Doug was sitting over on the sofa in the cottage, the left side of his face red around the eye and cheek where Stu had hit him. He was unconsciously clenching and unclenching his fist, thinking thoughts that distorted his lips – but he was holding his anger successfully for the moment, holding tightly onto his greater ulterior aim.

"I found the address," Stu said as he walked quickly across from the kitchen area of the cottage.

"That was our best chance back there, you're a total idiot," Doug growled.

"What, you were going to just manhandle her into the car right in front of all those people?"

"They were too far away to see much — and what now? You think we're going to just drive up to some cop's house and snatch her?"

"Yeah, and do it cool, not with bully tactics."

"And where's Dana gone?"

"I don't know. I think she's run off somewhere. She knows she gets a cut," Stuart said. "She's no fool."

"You're too soft and fat for operations like this."

"I was in Nam just like you — if the cop's not there with her cowboy, we go in and grab them quiet and easy, get this thing done in the next hour — he'll talk if we bang her a bit — tough enough for you, tough guy? Then we head right over to Oakland, make the deal and then head out."

"And if the cop's up at the house?"

"We wait our chance."

"Not my style."

"So I've noticed."

"Almost certainly a .22-short bullet, about four or five feet away. No sign yet of the pistol. This probably happened maybe around midnight from the looks if it all, we'll know more after the autopsy."

Kate stared down at Reggie Davis lying there in his own blood, mostly just stained dirt now that had puddled around his head. "No chance of a suicide?" she asked just to be sure.

"No powder burns. And no gun."

"His wallet?"

"Thrown on the ground beside him, money gone if there was any. Student ID was there, that's why we phoned, you had something similar Sunday night, right?"

"Yeah. Okay, thanks Don. Keep me in the loop."

"No problem, old time's sake, I owed you one. You're missed over here, you know that."

Ty spoke up. "Another question – any link to a car?"

"Two possibles parked on the street there – it's a tow-away zone after 6 am."

"Make and model?"

"One's a '63 Ford Fairlane, the other's a late-model BMW sedan, don't know the year yet."

"Damn," Ty said. "I was hoping for a Chevrolet."

They walked away from the crime scene, pushing through gawkers. "Let's get back quick," Kate said, "ask around campus about that blue Bel Air the old woman saw. I just can't get my mind around this."

"Well maybe I can," he said. "I told you I chatted with that Watts guy just now."

"So?"

"Reggie was one of the foursome, right? Jon, Stuart, Reggie and Doug."

"And Paul."

"So we have two of five down. Jon didn't do this, so that leaves Stuart and Douglas. I suspect Doug is our man. You interviewed him, what did you find?"

"Smooth as ice – but when Paul was shot Doug claims he was together with about ten other students at the singles dorm."

"Well that guy Watts fingered him."

"What – why?"

"Just a hunch – you have that radio phone, call your house and tell the kids to stay put. Better still, tell them to drive to some public place – we'll meet them there. I don't like coincidences, especially when lined up in a row – same tight little group, same type gun, same distance from shooter to forehead. Where was Stuart when Paul went down?"

"He says he was out driving – no witnesses. And what about that dead minister, she limps and she had a motive – blasphemy, playing God. And those kids were working together, not against each other."

"Hey, several million bucks wholesale for those quart-bottles of pure LSD – that strikes me as a motive, I've known people getting shot for nickels and dimes."

"But – Jon isn't telling anybody where those bottles are, is he?"

"That's what he said but I can't give you a hundred percent on that. He's damn fervent against the war. Would he do it for money? No. But to save the world from its defunct elders – maybe. You said he was picked up at the jail by who exactly?"

"Stuart, Douglas and Dana."

"Well goddamn – phone!"

She did. It rang. And rang. And rang.

"Try both the cottages – you have the numbers?"

She did. Again – no answer.

27

For once Stuart himself was driving his old Plymouth, the steering wheel rubbing against his hefty belly. Doug was headed off somewhere in his VW camper, holding Julia as human sacrifice if Jonathan, who was sitting tensely in Stuart's passenger seat, didn't come forth now with the Sandoz bottles. Jon had a dark rivulet of drying blood under his left nostril where he'd been socked just moments after Stuart and Douglas entered the cop woman's premises. He'd made a quick defensive reaction to the intrusion and Douglas had popped him fast and accurately but not too hard to cause problems with their plans.

"You're being a total idiot, you know that," Jon now growled at Stuart, who was driving with tense shoulders and his lips even tighter. "Kidnapping is lethal in court, for both of you. You can stop this right now, just turn around and – "

"Shut up!"

"You don't even have a gun, I could jump you."

They were dropping down into San Anselmo, turning onto Ross, headed for the seminary. Stuart was wearing a jacket. With one hand he tapped his left side. "Right here."

"Get serious - you're not fool enough to use it. What's with you, what are you on, have you gone completely insane?"

"Not me, but Douglas, he's definitely a bit extreme. I had to hit him myself, earlier. That's probably why he punched you for no reason."

"And him off with Julia – I'll kill you if he does anything."

Stuart looked right in Jon's eyes. "I have no control over any of this right now. If I don't make that phone call from the pay booth over at Safeway at exactly one o'clock, as you heard Doug insist, then who knows what he'll do to Julia. It's all up to you – get me those bottles with no time lost, or she's cooked."

"And you two just ride off into the sunset?"

"We stay here like nothing happened, at least until the situation heats up across the bay."

"What – you let me go and I go tell the cops?"

"You say one word to anybody at all and Julia. she'll be dead meat. Doug doesn't mind killing, I found that out."

"Meaning what?"

"Nothing. You just get me those bottles, then you'll get Julia back and forever we all keep our little secret. What proof would you have anyway?"

They were turning right, into the Seminary. Jon was so tense he was hardly breathing at all. The last he'd seen of Julia was her head disappearing through the side door of Doug's VW camper.

She'd in fact just been given a parallel deadly lecture – that if she misbehaved, her lover boy would be shot. There was really nothing either of them could do but play along. But Julia was trying to keep track of where they were driving as they headed up and up and up a back road on Mount Tam. Douglas noticed her quick looks, pulled over to the side of the road and turned off the engine. "Get in back," he ordered her.

"And if I say no?" she retorted, seriously afraid of the man but determined to play tough.

"Two things are quite easy for me to do. I clobber you and fuck you and otherwise demonstrate that you are in my power. And at the end of all this I cut off your lover boy's balls and fry them in a nice garlic batter. Either's fine with me – or both."

She hesitated just a moment – then got up and went between the two front seats into the back. "Lay down on the bed on your back with your hands on those lovely breasts of yours. Good. Now raise your head, yes, good little girl."

He tied the red bandana he'd worn the night before tightly around her head over her eyes. He tied her hands with another bandana he'd bought – then he moved his hands down onto her breasts and relished the pure sensation of those firm nuggets. She kept her mouth shut and went stiff as a board. He let his hands move down all over her, squeezing and pushing wherever he wanted to – but she remained frozen. Not much fun – he'd return to this morsel later. Time to drive the rest of the way, deposit her properly and await the call.

Stuart drove up the Seminary back drive and parked down below the redwoods below the cottages. Jon got stiffly out of the Plymouth. Stuart did likewise, huffing and puffing, taking out the pistol. Jon glanced around – there was no one in sight, just those three Seminary staff houses up to the left a ways off. Stuart motioned with the pistol and Jon started walking up the path from the lower road as if going to his cottage like he'd done a hundred times in the past few months.

Then at a particular giant redwood tree he hung a right and started making his way perpendicular to the path through the overgrown underbrush. Stuart came right behind him and a couple times Jon let a branch snap back and slap the guy in the face – but he knew that if Stuart didn't make that phone call, Julia would be in terrible trouble, so he put all thought of successful counter-attack out of his mind.

He counted. One tree, two, three, stop. It was so shady here, deep in the redwoods. And totally quiet. Jon had come down here often all alone when his wife had started complaining about everything, just before she left. A breeze was moving through the tops of the trees hundreds of feet above but down here there was no breeze at all.

Something moved behind and to the left of them and Stuart swung around quick, the pistol out in the open in his left hand. "Chipmunk," Jon told him. "You're a wreck, Stu. Put that damn thing away."

"Where's those bottles – come on!"

"Let me get my bearings. Ah, I remember now, somewhere over here I think."

"You think! You don't even have a map or anything? You could just forget and there would go the whole thing."

"You really believe that this acid is actually going to change anything in the world?"

"Damn right – it's pure power. Spirit power."

"You're talking spirit with a gun in your hand."

"You just don't get it, do you," Stuart grumbled.

"What I get is that you think you can use violence to beget peace. Good luck there."

"We've got a war being fought here."

"War between you and me? Will you actually shoot me if I don't give you the acid? You're being a total numbskull shit."

"You've gotta understand, we're in way too deep on several fronts to change course now. Douglas will carry forth even if I falter. And I'm not faltering – this is holy work and time's ticking. Get me the stuff."

With Stuart standing alert with his pistol about twenty feet away, Jon walked over and reached down into the deep hollow between two downed trees, feeling damp cool green moss – then sure enough, his fingers came upon glass.

"Ah, found them, both of them!" he shouted.

"Keep your voice down," Stu mumbled back. "Bring 'em out and be careful, don't break the damn things or we're both shot."

Jon came walking back, gripping the neck of a quart jar in each hand, doing his best not to stumble in the shadows as he worked his way over and through downed trees and branches. He was ten feet from Stuart when a voice shouted loud and clear from the direction of the path:

"Freeze – police!"

"Uhm – Dad?" Jon intoned.

Stuart saw the cowboy standing there some distance away in the shadows, pistol aimed at Stuart's chest. Stuart had his own pistol, aimed right at Jon but at a much closer distance.

"You fire at me, I swear I'll get your son first," he said to Ty. "Drop your gun or I fire on the count of three. One … two …"

"Okay, ease up," Ty said, letting his gun fall into the redwood needles.

"Now you walk real slow toward me."

Ty walked real slow.

"Sit down right there."

Ty eyed him, considered saying something, looking for an edge – but stayed silent and sat.

"Fuck it all," Stuart muttered at him, his voice extreme. "Now you've gone and made this real serious. Fucking idiot! What am I supposed to do now, shoot you both? Where's that sexy cop friend of yours?"

"Unfortunately still up at her house looking for clues," Ty told him, "or you'd be down flat right now. That was a quick move you made, for a fat seminary student."

"Basic 'Nam reaction. Shit, I can't believe it's down to this – Jon, get over there by your dad – now!"

At the exact moment he said 'now' there came a sudden loud crack of a gunshot that echoed in the redwoods as a bullet tore into his right shoulder. He stumbled to the side and fell to the ground, the pistol dropping from his hand.

Ty was immediately on his feet, moving fast to go grab the gun.

Out of the shadows stepped – agent Thomas.

"Cut it, Hadley. Put the gun down."

"So the CIA finally does something worthwhile," Ty muttered, an edge of relief to his voice. "I never thought I'd be glad to see your ugly mug. How'd you know about this?"

"The old lady at the house down there, same one you talked to a bit earlier than me – she'd kindly agreed to phone me immediately if she saw anything suspicious. As serendipity would have it, I just happened to be in the neighborhood." Thomas walked over closer to Jon. "Well well. Might you just possibly be holding exactly what I'm out here on assignment to obtain and destroy?"

"That remains to be seen," Jon said back.

Stuart was making a noise – Thomas went over and quickly checked him out. "Just a flesh wound, you're not going to die," Thomas growled at him. "I could have taken you out and saved the tax payer a lot of money. Shut up or I'll put another hole in you."

Jon was feeling suddenly light-headed, not able to concentrate. He knew that if he told the agent about the kidnapping, they might push Douglas into hurting Julia – but if he didn't tell him, what then? Suddenly everything seemed still and clear in his head. "So you want to destroy these?" he asked, holding up the two bottles.

"Damn right I do. That shit is the plague of our age. At least we'll take that much out of circulation."

"Well then allow me to do the dirty deed," Jon said. He cocked an arm and tossed one of the bottles hard through the air at the trunk of a nearby tree – it shattered in a liquid explosion that represented enough LSD to get every ant within a thousand miles high as a kite.

"Now that was most obliging," Thomas said. "I think I'm going to get along with you much better than I do with your father here."

Jonathan just nodded with a smile – then twisted off the cap of the other bottle and tipped it up like a wine bottle and started drinking the liquid, glug glug glug.

"Jon – stop!" his father shouted at him, starting to move toward the drinker – but Thomas stepped in front of him with pistol ready to shoot.

"Let the boy do what he wants," he ordered. "This is most amusing."

Jon was still drinking, now deep into his cups. Finally he stopped, lowered the bottle. He'd drunk at least a quarter of its contents. "Ah," he said. "That should be enough LSD to get me as high as these trees here, wouldn't you say?"

"You must know," Thomas reminded him, "that less than tenth of an ounce of pure LSD guarantees death within minutes. Says so right on the bottle – undiluted it's poison. Even contact with the skin of that amount is enough to stop your heart."

"Goddamn Jon!" Ty shouted.

Jon just grinned, raised the bottle up over his head and poured the liquid down upon his face in a small waterfall of splashy psychedelica. Then he tossed the half-empty bottle against the same redwood trunk – the bottle shattered and that was that.

Everyone was silent for a moment. Ty was so utterly stunned he couldn't speak. Meanwhile birds overhead were singing away like it was the first day of the rest of their blessed lives. A small patch of needles right in front of Jon was being brightly illuminated by a single shaft of sunlight making it's way down to the forest floor.

Jon suddenly popped out of his blank inner state, saw Stuart down on the ground, remembered Julia and leapt into a decision. "Hey, come on, Dad – we gotta get Stuart up out of here," he said urgently. "Douglas has Julia, he's threatening to kill her, Stuart has to make a phone call in about twenty minutes from Safeway or Doug does who knows what to her, he's a maniac."

"Kidnapping?" Thomas asked.

"Yeah but I've got no idea where he is – this is the shits, and Stuart has to make that phone call!"

"But Goddamn, Jon," Ty said, pushing to the fore. "The acid!"

"We tried the stuff months ago, somebody at the Institute played games on somebody – it's just plain water. Wouldn't get a fly high."

He hurried over to where Stuart was lying on the ground. "Come on, Stu, let's move!"

That would have been an excellent idea considering the circumstances – except that Stuart wasn't moving. He was still breathing, but he'd slipped unconscious.

28

The camper van swayed and bounced its way out of San Anselmo and far up the slopes of Mount Tamalpais. Her inner experience of forced blindness and tightly-tied wrists was almost more than she could take – she wanted to scratch out the eyes of her captor. Knowing he was occupied with driving, she managed to sit up cross-legged so that she wouldn't get sick to her stomach. This was so bizarre – she'd known this guy for four months now, and although she'd never at all warmed to him, she'd never imagined he was this crazy.

Her mind tried to think straight and get ready to do something to get free from him, but all she could focus on was the pain down in her wrists with the bandana over-tight and the memory of the guy's menacing fingers squeezing her breasts like they were his to touch and then sliding down to her lower sexual regions with obvious future intent – and right then she got caught in a flood of buried memories of Uncle Earl slapping her in the face and then the whole avalanche of memories of what had happened after that …

The VW came to an abrupt stop but she was such an emotional basket-case right then that she hardly noticed the cessation of movement and sudden silence when the engine went dead. She just sat there hunched over, breathing with half-sobs through her mouth, wanting to go unconscious and escape reality altogether.

Her right arm was suddenly grabbed, but not as violently as before. "Okay my lovely, out we go," he said to her, his tone actually almost normal now.

"Take this off," she muttered, referring to the bandana covering her eyes

"Let's get inside first, come along now."

He helped her rather gently to step down out of the camper. Ah, the air smelled sharp and good, loads of eucalyptus and some other scents she couldn't discriminate one from the other. A soft breeze hit her hot face like a blessed touch. There were no sounds of cars or people – just a few birds singing off in the distance.

He led her by the arm along a grassy walkway. Still blind, wearing shorts and sneakers, she felt suddenly grounded down into her feet. They went up three steps onto a stone or cement porch and then on into a cool room. The bandana came off, he untied her hands and there she was, standing in a rather stark but bright living room in a small modern ranch house.

"Welcome to my little hideaway from the noxious world below," he said, walking over to the open kitchen area and putting a pot of water on the stove. "Coffee?"

"Coffee – yes. What is this place – yours?" she asked, hungry for any semblance of normalcy.

"Government checks cover the rent," he told her. "Have a seat, please, you are my guest."

"Doug, are you totally schizoid, changing faces every five minutes?"

He smiled at that. "It serves a man to have several faces with which to greet the chaos of the world. Please, do make yourself comfortable."

"That's not how criminals talk to kidnap victims."

"I much prefer to see this little jaunt as a business junket that we're both going to benefit considerably from."

"You can't play these games and not go to jail – you're definitely crazy."

"Perceive closely who's in charge here, who's totally masterminding this maneuver. I am the opposite of insane, I am absolutely brilliant. You'll do best to see your presence here in the same light that I do. Now sit."

She sat.

The sofa had a chromium frame like the other furniture in the room. Floor was hardwood. The house sat atop a canyon ridge, no other house in sight. A giant glass window and sliding glass door looked out over a spectacular view of Fairfax, San Anselmo and Ross far below.

"What do you mean, the government pays for this, a pension?" she said, wanting to keep chatter going rather than the silence that had come over them as he sat in a separate easy chair and stared off at the detached world far below.

He turned his head and stared at her a moment as if not quite present. Then he spoke in a terse tone. "No more questions This is a business transaction. My intent is to quickly acquire considerable wealth, then exit the scene. This is my due that the government failed to provide. You don't actually think that I would become a fawning minister of the faith – I mean, really."

He paused, awaiting an answer from her. "I have no idea," she mumbled.

"The hippie freaks are right about one thing – there is indeed a flow to life. In a few hours I'll have a million dollars in my pocket. And at even the slightest suspicion of your approaching the police or the CIA –

actually I could just as easily shoot you right here and now. But that would draw flies and besides I am at heart a generous person, I might even give your lover boy fifty thousand dollars, to make him criminally involved."

"We don't want money – take the LSD and go."

"Yes, well. That depends on whether that phone on the counter rings properly on time. No ring from Stuart at one sharp – you're history. That was my bargain with Jon and I stand by it."

He walked with his slight but constant limp over to the kitchen area where he started making coffee. "Milk and sugar, a bit of chocolate perhaps?" he offered, shifting into friendly mode again. "Stuart taught me this one thing – how to make a superior cup of coffee."

"You two were planning this all along?"

"Stuart is a bother – he'll be gone quite soon."

Her breathing froze as she realized that this man must have been the one who shot Paul. She stood up, panicked, her body on fire. With an explosion of spontaneous energy she turned and took off running out of the room toward the front door, her sneakers slapping loudly against the floor.

She made it to the door and grabbed the knob and twisted – but he was behind her grabbing roughly, pulling her against him from the back, squeezing her breasts painfully. She struggled, tried to hit and kick him – but his muscles were like iron and his grip made her cry out helplessly in bruised pain.

"That was not wise," he said at her in a nasty tone of voice. "I thought we were going to be friends. I was even thinking that perhaps we could go off together. You are such a morsel. Mm. Feel those!"

"Let me go!"

And just like that, he actually did let her go – stepping back and ogling her visual presence with obvious pleasure. "Ah, I do like the wild ones," he said matter-of-factly. "And rest assured, this house is entirely fail-safe. No one has ever escaped."

"You're the killer," she bellowed at him. "You shot my husband!"

"Why does everyone keep accusing me of doing such a thing. What would be my motive, after all? I do not perform random acts of violence, thank you – except in the privacy of my own home. So I also continue wondering who it was that had enough nerve, in a quite placid seminary community no less, to amble over to Paul's cottage and pull that trigger. No, I did not put the Savior down, even though I would have no difficulty doing such a job. That was what 'Nam was all about. So then – coffee?"

She sat numb, sipping coffee, sitting there in the living room locked up with this maniac. The clock on the kitchen wall said twelve forty-three. She could hear it clicking away the moments. He was silent again, seeming to have a habit of staring over the abyss outside his window as if she wasn't even there – indeed as if he himself wasn't there. All she could think about were the karate classes she was taking down at the San Rafael Y – but she doubted she could actually bring herself to use what she'd learned.

Suddenly Douglas was active again, socially-charged. "It wasn't entirely pure chance that I came to the Seminary," he said to her out of the blue as if continuing a previous conversation. "My momma, she was quite religious, she used to deliver constant and rather nasty punishment in the name of the Lord, there was the Devil everywhere in her world, especially right deep inside me. And then as if a gift from God on high, in the first miracle in my life I was rescued by a teacher who noticed too many bruises once too often and they took dear old Mums away. And because I was so brainy I ended up with a scholarship to Memphis U. Are you listening?"

"Uhm – yes. Yes."

"At college I found it quite easy to mimic people and eliminate my rural hillbilly twang. Psychology fascinated me and still does. More coffee? I never keep food here – I prefer to fast when I come up, keeps the mind clear. Hitler was a vegetarian you know. He wasn't crazy either, just overly wired on speed. I actually came to Seminary because I wanted to find out the truth about good and evil. Taking on my CIA spy job there was a paid passport, I played those fools without breaking a sweat, still do. And guess what – the more I look for the Devil at the Seminary the more I realize that evil was pure and simple a grand idea invented by the priestly cult way back when to maintain covert fear-based control of the masses. And to be sure, my religious pilot buddies claimed they were justified by God in what they were doing in Nam – frying geeks for Christ, napalming the Commies to hell and gone."

He stopped talking, stared into space a long moment. Julia was calculating the odds that the big plate-glass window of the living room would shatter if she could manage to throw a chair through it.

"After all the shit that I did in 'Nam," he was saying, "and then left laying around in a fucking Vet hospital in Virginia, there was no way for me to move forward in life but try and make peace with the Devil so I could get on with some fun – so imagine my surprise when I got out here and discovered that there's just no such thing as evil and hell and brimstone and all the rest – we just do what we want to do and then we die and that's that. Oops, look there," he said, smiling, eyeing the clock. "Almost High Noon. Tick tick tick."

Julia looked over at the clock.

"In either case, Stuart must go," his voice continued. "I've been swallowing his holier than thou shit for three long months now – he's going to take it right up the ass. Pardon my French."

"I need to go to the bathroom," Julia told him.

"What?"

"I'm going to pee in my pants."

"Oh – of course. Want some help?"

She stood up. "Just tell me where it is."

"Down the hall where such bathrooms always are, these American architects are so goddamn dumb and boring. Of course there's no way for you to escape, don't even try or I might lose my friendly edge, I'm doing my best to be friendly here, I hope you're appreciating the effort. Small talk and all the rest. I never was good at small talk."

There was no lock on the bathroom door. There was a window but not big enough for her to get through. She remembered the intruder in Jon's cottage – ah, had that been Doug too?

She peed for a very long time. She must have spaced out sitting there on the toilet. When she came back into the living room he was just sitting there. She looked at the clock and it said one oh two. "They could have run into trouble," she said at him, her voice shaky. "The police were all over the campus."

He didn't respond. She sat down. He was flexing his biceps, first the right one, then the left, just slightly, unconsciously like a nervous tick. He was only a few inches taller than she was, but she guessed that he outweighed her by fifty pounds and most of that muscle.

"Jonathan won't let me down," she told him.

"That wimp? You don't know shit – and I need that cash, you understand? I got my Bali hide-away set for a lifetime of nasty fun, I'm not spending another stinking night at that fucking seminary. They phone right now or I'm blowing this lid sky high – I'm way overdue."

"But, there could be something wrong with the phone and – "

"Shut up. Get that dandy little tight girly ass you're always wagging in my face into the bedroom right now – move!"

"No! You are not going to abuse me. I'll die first"

He stood up with a quick spring-like reflex of his body and the next instant he was towering over her. "I'm going to do what I damn well want – morsel like you, no way I'm not eating. Get into that bedroom and get your boobs and ass out of those clothes if you don't want me ripping them off. And make yourself nice and slippery and open wide or I'll be ripping you open the hard way."

She didn't move.

With a sudden swift swipe of his hand he slapped her face hard, knocking her back against the couch.

Stunned, she tasted her own blood. He yanked her up onto her feet and pushed her violently toward the hallway. She stumbled, fell to the floor hard – regained her footing and went on numbly toward the bedroom.

"Tell you what I'll do, to be fair and all. I give them three more minutes," he shouted after her. "And hear me clear – I want you stripped down to skin when I come in. Look at this, you already got me hard."

She blindly through her tears found the bedroom and opened the door, slamming it shut behind her. N o lock on her side. And just a single mattress on the floor, blankets and pillows and clothes thrown all around, nasty smell in the air. She opened the two windows but they opened only about three inches on their sliders and that was that.

So she just stood looking down at the bed for a long blank moment – and then went into action. She sat down and started taking off her shoes, slowly unlacing each one as she sat on the edge of the mattress. Then she pulled off her shirt and sat there holding her breasts in her hands, trying to bring Jonathan to mind, trying to call out to him for help, to anyone for help. God, help me. Help me. God.

But as is so often the case in real life, instead of God to the rescue, a few minutes later the devil appeared. Douglas came into the room fast and closed the door behind him. He looked down at the mattress and with a reflexive grin, saw what he most wanted to see, loads of bare young female skin and wide-open thighs, pubic hair and hands down sexy as could be between her legs like the real slut he'd all along figured her for – and the sight turned him on so hard he was ripping at his clothes to get them off, staggering around on one foot pulling at a sock, yanking down his Jockey shorts, half ripping them in the process, his purple penis bursting throbbing into the open dank sex-room air.

And yes, it was all in the end so simple. He just came right down onto her with his whole weight and she just came right up at him at the same instant with her knuckles in precision attack position as she swung her left arm and smashed her fist right into his face, seriously crushing his nose and splintering interior bones and thus shocking his nervous system so thoroughly that he managed only one visceral wholebody spasm before he collapsed down with his full limp weight onto her.

29

Later that day as the sun was setting, Tyson Hadley was alone in Kate's kitchen with a big super-sharp knife in his hand – a Japanese-style masterpiece that cut veggies like magic. The wine he was drinking was some local Napa red that made him want to drink the whole bottle. His son meanwhile was out in the hot tub indulging in his second boiled-lobster experience of the day ... and there was a naked and luckily-alive young woman also in that hot water. Ty didn't know if it was the onions or Julia being alive that had a tough cowboy like him actually a bit blurry in the eyes, thinking back over the day and wondering if there really was a God who could interfere with human events in favor of the good guys.

The front door opened and shut with a slight slam. Footsteps behind – then arms going around him. "How'd it end up?" he asked, putting the knife down and turning around to face her.

"It's always a mess when the CIA butts in but we're done for now. They have Doug under guard at the hospital. I don't know if he's conscious. How are you?"

"Able to breathe again. Doing up some enchiladas and such for dinner. That wine's great, want some?"

He poured her a glass, not waiting for an answer.

"And Julia?" she asked before they raised glasses to a conjoined click.

"Hot tub with Jon."

"Whew. And I see you found my one good knife."

"From Japan I assume, judging from the way it looks and cuts."

"Actually it was forged by an American named Frank Richtig from Nebraska, a couple generations ago."

"Cuts as good as Japanese and they make the best."

"Oh, the Turks and thereabouts way back when, they made knives and swords just as good – they cut right through Crusader steel."

Ty put down his wine, picked up the knife again. "Hm. The woodwork on the handle, I guess that's not quite Japanese style."

"It's one of the few things besides this house that I insisted on keeping in the divorce. Do all cowboys know Japanese cutlery?"

"I'm a bit of a blade-smith, tinker with alloys and such. Real pros do it twelve hours every day, I do knives and woodwork a few months each winter."

"You do keep busy out there in the wilderness."

"Might as well."

"I'm sure there's plenty of cowgirls around to fill your spare time when the cold winds blow."

"I'm a bit picky when it comes to such things. I saw the for sale sign on your lawn – what's that all about?"

"I'm in escrow."

"Moving somewhere?"

"Out," she said.

"What about your job?"

"I'm done on the first. Time to fly."

"Where to?"

"Several possibilities."

"What are you going off to do?"

"Finish a book," she said.

"Book about what?"

"My ex – corporate corruption. Going to need my full attention for a couple months to get it finished."

"I've got an extra room down home – half a dozen in fact. Plenty of peace and quiet."

"Look out what you offer."

"Always do."

They fell silent a moment. Sipped wine.

"I'll help you get those enchiladas into the oven," she offered, "so we can go get naked in the tub with the kids."

"I'm not getting naked into any hippie tub in front of my own son," he reacted. "Thanks anyway."

"This is San Francisco, Ty, not Cambria."

"Hey, Jon's probably never seen me without clothes on."

"Now that's real cowboy. Maybe it's time to go urban on that front. I'll grate some cheese."

"Done – in the fridge."

"Chop the olives," she offered.

"Likewise – we're all set to roll and bake. You a good enchy-roller?"

"Is the Pope a good confessor?"

"Remains to be seen."

"Ty, I challenge you to transcend false modesty and join us in the tub. Prove you possess true courage, packin' real huevos Cuyamos."

"You mean sans clothes?"

"That's how it's done up here in civilization."

"I'd say you're pushing me a bit hard on this one."

She grinned. "I like you hard. I'm pushing you toward the true pleasures of life."

"I'm a real bashful cowpoke."

"Time to get you over it."

"You're serious about this – challenging me right where you know I'm scared."

"Just provoking the tiger. Looking for your limits. Goofing around with your rigid parts."

The surface of the water had become so calm it was now glass between them. She had her eyes closed and hardly seemed to be breathing. Their feet were slightly touching down below. He felt languid, at peace inside his own skin – just the opposite of how he'd felt four hours ago down at the police station as the cops took forever to initiate a search for the VW camper, their first and only lead considering that Stuart was still unconscious in the hospital, having lost a lot more blood than the CIA agent had assumed.

Then, just as cop cars from every station in Marin County were set to roar off in search of Doug's camper van, that same machine had come roaring down Ross Avenue right into the police parking lot, brakes slamming to a jolting stop – and Julia had come jumping out, running across the lot right into Jon's arms, sobbing her eyes out, shaking and then going limp in his grip.

Now she was at least partly recovered. Her eyes opened – big brown lobes of stillness with infinite black interiors. He could see himself somewhat in the candle-light reflection of her cornea.

She blinked.

"Maybe we've about had enough of this liquid heat," he said.

"But my mind – I still just can't remember – anything."

"Maybe best to just let it go."

"I just want to go off forever, sand away at a big beautiful piece of mahogany, sand and saw and saw and sand – I want to leave all this and go away where I can just be caught up entirely with wood – and you – and not ever ever think back."

"So that's easy, perfect – we've got a great woodworking shop set up down at the ranch, my dad does projects all winter, you'd fit right in. Saw and sand and fun stuff all in between – I've also decided to split this place, go help Dad a bit. Both my cousins are gone from down there now, he needs help – and Alan was telling me a while back that I can get a draft deferment for agriculture work."

"What – would you really actually want to just take me in?" She met his eyes, her expression starting to soften. But just then something caught her eye, she looked suddenly up and behind him toward the doorway into the house.

Jon turned his head. Kate stood there as naked as the day she was born with towel casually in hand. And what? There was Ty standing half hiding behind her looking downright sheepish but determined not to bolt and run, sporting various exposed expanses of baby-white cowboy skin contrasting against his deeply-tanned neck and forearms. A towel was wrapped securely around his middle regions, held up by a tight fist.

"Mind if we join you?" Kate asked.

Julia stood up from the water.

"We're just getting out," Jon said, holding her hand as she stepped up and out. Ty tried to avert his eyes.

"Well, the great Tyson Hadley," his son jibed at him, "getting stark naked into a hot tub. Now I've seen about everything."

"Not quite yet – get off with you," Ty said right back. "Enchiladas and salad and tidbits almost ready. Be there or be square."

There are few things a traditional country boy fears more than somebody seeing him out in public with an erection threatening to grow out of control in response to the visual stimulation of an alluring female. The delicious curves of Kate's naked back and derriere as he'd followed her outside and now the utter breath-taking magnificence of Julia rising up out of the tub definitely threatened to set off Ty's internal plumbing and that was the ultimate taboo, getting a hard-on right in front of your own kid's girlfriend.

Thus it was that Ty proceeded to move his body splashing fast down into the water. He almost bellowed like a stuck pig as his penis got boiled alive in water so goddarn hot he feared for his entire future virility –

Meanwhile, as Jon and Julia disappeared into the house, Kate stepped calmly into that same water without so much as a single twinge of pain, and soon thereafter Ty realized he wasn't going to die – in fact he was soon half-floating into an extended moment of pure sensory pleasure. "Ah, must be just like the womb," he said.

"You've really never been in a hot tub before?"

"No self-respecting ranch has a hippie hot tub – but this feels damn good."

"We'll load this into your pickup as my first contribution to your back porch – assuming you're serious about asking me to visit your turf. And hey mister," she said in a mock-accusatory tone, "what's that burly beast you got growing down there? If you hadn't left your cowboy hat inside, you could just nonchalantly drop it right in the water and cover up all that forbidden bulge of lusty manhood."

"You must write awful purty prose, talking like you do about the unspeakables."

Their eyes locked in mutual emotion. "Ah Tyson," she muttered low to him. "I don't want you ever to go away, not without me."

"So pack up and come with me."

"Just like that?"

"Just like that."

Right at that intimate moment a gruff intruding masculine voice spoke up behind him. "And so, they rode off into the sunset – most romantic."

Ty jolted upright as if poked with his own cattle prod. His head spun around as he fumbled for the pistol he'd forgotten to bring outside. Thomas stood ten feet from them, silhouetted in the open back door of the house. "Well goddamn you," Ty growled at him, "you do that kind of trick one more time and you'll suck a bullet – what the fuck you mean breaking in here? This time I'm calling the cops."

"I observe several cops already here – and for the record I was let in the front door by a polite young man who told me where to find you. No laws broken." He walked over toward the tub, looking down at them, as usual dressed prim in coat and tie and black shoes.

"Come on in why don't you," Kate offered.

"Now hold on," Ty reacted. "This might be San Francisco but I'm not sharing water with no CIA agent."

"Luckily I concur," Thomas said. "But we do have some talking to get done and I've got less than an hour before I head off for Berkeley."

"Then please," Kate said, "go inside and ask Jon to pour you some wine or whiskey or whatever you like from the bar in the living room. You can join us for dinner, we can talk then."

Thomas shrugged his shoulders. "I'm officially off-duty – don't mind if I do, thanks."

He disappeared back into the house. Kate eyed Ty's expression. "What's that look?" she asked curtly.

"There's the distinct possibility he's the one who killed Paul – he's as good a suspect, him or one of his fed thugs, as anybody else at this point. We haven't solved that case just because Douglas got arrested for kidnapping. I don't want that guy running loose in this house, sitting down for dinner with us like he's family."

"It's the wise move," she intoned. "Keep in close contact with the enemy, if indeed he killed Paul. But there's still a chance the minister might have done the killing, she had a motive, religiously neurotic as it might sound, plus access and means. So perhaps did Stuart. For that matter we still don't know about Dana, or perhaps some New York thug. So – I invited Agent Thomas to dinner because something's gotta give."

Ty exhaled loud into the steamy air. "What a mess. When I read murder mysteries, they make all this police procedure look so fast and easy and successful – but real life, on all fronts, just doesn't happen like that."

"So I've noticed."

His eyes dropped down to look at her presence underwater for just a second and then back up fast, but she noticed. "Usually the sex isn't half as good in real life either," she said, raising her hands to modestly cover her mammary abundance.

"At least we can do something about that." He leaned forward and kissed her with a flair of passion.

"Hey – some shy cowboy you are."

He proceeded to make a slippery move with both hands, pulling her toward him so that they were in a rather intimate posture deeper down in the silky-soft depths of the water.

"Ah – but Ty, stop – the kids are right inside there and that CIA agent's probably spying on us."

"Now who's being the shy cowboy? Uhm … Ahh. I'm starting to like these here hot tubs."

30

Taking more time to get dressed than Jon had, Julia had been alone in the downstairs bedroom pulling on her underwear when she heard the front door ring and Jon admit that slimy CIA agent into the house – the same pushy jerk she'd had to deal with down at the police station a few hours earlier. For no overt reason she felt threatened and angry, shaky in her knees, as Jonathan hesitantly let the guy enter and ask for Kate, then walk on down the hallway, past her slightly-open bedroom door and out into the back yard to Ty and Kate in the tub.

As she finished dressing for dinner, she heard the agent come back into the living room and Jon reluctantly offer him a drink as Kate had suggested. Without thinking she went into high alert, creeping forward down the hallway toward the living room to where she could listen without being seen.

Jonathan meanwhile was still feeling slightly euphoric from his recent erogenous wine-imbued encounter. But deep down in his gut, as he stood face to face with the CIA agent, he remembered that Paul's killer was still at large – perhaps this guy was the one who'd pulled the trigger. Without forethought he decided to play at his Dad's game, standing with the suited agent calmly before the fire his father had built, sipping a whiskey with the agent even though Jon hated whiskey.

"So at least you're out of jail," agent Tom said.

"For now," Jon responded evenly.

"That was damn lucky, your girlfriend escaping like she did from that guy. Cute number you got there."

"Cute number? You married?"

"Hey, I reviewed your career stats, you're a super smart guy, what's your career trajectory, you don't strike me as the minister type."

"If I can avoid the draft I'll do grad work at Stanford, maybe figure out why people like you agree to take on jobs that are violent and immoral."

"We were all set to nail you for terrorist activity — would've been your ass if you'd dumped all that LSD in the government water supply."

"Maybe I put a few drops in your whisky," Jon reacted, his voice rising, "straighten out at least one bent CIA brain."

"Ease up, I'm not the enemy here — my job is to help America stay free and strong and healthy. I do respect you for thusfar holding back with the acid. Where is it by the way?"

"You saw me drink it — nothing but tap water."

"You're maybe too smart for your own good. You know what a terrorist charge will get you?"

"Speaking of terrorist activity, I studied all the '50s covert CIA activity in Central America, how far you guys push your anti-Commie murder routine — and now here you are, violating our basic American rights to religious freedom and spiritual exploration."

"You are not by any stretch of the constitution, free to hook American kids on mind-deranging drugs."

"Alan Watts told me just last week," Jon retorted, "about your very own plans to dump thousands of acid tabs laced with speed onto the street in Berkeley."

"Well I know Alan, he's a blabber mouth who doesn't know his professional ass from a holy hole in the ground, pardon the French."

"It's clear that you yourself are the enemy you claim to be hunting – criminally interfering with America's urgently-needed spiritual wake-up."

"You seem to quote Lord Alan non-stop. Don't you have anything original to say?" He finished his whiskey, poured himself another and then refilled Jon's glass. "With all that LSD research you did at that Institute back east, you surely realize that LSD in any form is a dangerous drug with potentially-deadly downsides."

"I agree with Dr. Osmond – we need to set up legal centers in every state where people can take LSD under proper guidance and screening. Bobbie Kennedy privately supported that plan."

"And I say let's just leave God's most delicate neural creation alone."

"Well God's creation includes natural psychedelics like peyote and mushrooms and marijuana.. If you think God's natural wake-up process is un-American, then you're by definition an enemy of the people."

"Good boy, now you're quoting another obnoxious guy, Tim Leary. Shall I assume he's another hero of yours?"

"Leary's encouraging a spiritual revolution of the mind – just like Krishnamurti."

"Krishna who?" Thomas asked. "How do you spell his name?"

"Get out'a here."

"The Communists know that one of the best ways to take over a civilization is to get its youth so drugged and deluded they can't think straight."

"You'd rather we function as programmed robots in your grand capitalist machine – except for us radicals who you'd just as soon shoot dead in the street."

"My, you are on the radical horse."

"We have a constitutional right to do with our minds whatever we want. This is America the free – at least until you guys took over."

"I'm simply alerting you to the facts – if you aid and abet the Commie cause, turn our kids against America's values and damage their minds, then it's my job to stop you."

"By doing what, shooting people in the head?"

Jonathan watched for any subtle changes in the expression of the CIA agent. He saw none for a long moment – then he saw a slight twinkle in the man's cold blue eyes.

"That was nicely done," Thomas said. "Change your values and attitude and you'd make a good agent."

"Tell me, do you consider yourself a Christian?"

"I fighting for my faith every moment. What about you, Jon?"

"I do my best to avoid all pre-programmed beliefs – and that includes all the usual Christian models. We just want to think for ourselves for a change, rather than being forced to think the party line."

"You're again quoting your guru Mr. Watts."

"At least he's not like you, going off to 'Nam and napalming innocent women and children."

"So you'd rather wait for the Commies to slip into your cozy bedroom and murder your own kids. In order to survive, societies require strong moral backbone. Do you actually think Communism offers a better way?"

"Capitalism and Communism are both run by power-hungry bastards. War is good business, napalm a Commie for Christ. I'm looking for a better way – "

" – But you're looking through drugged-up eyes. I've been scraping LSD victims off American sidewalks for years. But enough of this, let's shift tone. I didn't come here to argue, I'm in fact here to work together with you, Jon – get you permanently off the hook for the murder of your friend."

"My guess is one of you guys put him down like you put down the Kennedys and Martin Luther King."

"Now you listen to me, kid. Your friend Paul was on our hot list for twenty-two months, he was a self-declared revolutionary out to destroy this country."

Jon was feeling suddenly out of gas, woozy from alcohol, shaky from arguing. "And I say total bull to all that – it's just your excuse for putting down dissent. Sure, you've got all your guns and money and phony morality that lets you murder innocent people without flinching – but in the end, you know deep down that we've got God on our side."

He downed the last of his whiskey, scowled at the agent of America's federal government, and walked out the sliding door to get some fresh air before dinner.

31

From her hidden vantage point Julia was able to watch Thomas as he stood there alone a moment, a swath of various emotions trying to gain hold on his face – but in the end just a cold blank frown emerged. As he went over to pour himself another drink she stepped back around the corner of the hallway – and ran right into the big chest of Jonathan's father.

"Oh," she whispered.

"Just checking on that guy," he whispered back, nodding toward the living room. He took her by the arm and walked her into the bedroom. The sliding glass door into the side yard and street was open and they could see Jonathan vaguely in the rising moon light, standing out there alone with his back to them.

"You doing okay?" Ty asked her softly.

"Oh – yes."

"How's the knuckles?"

"Bruised but nothing broken," she said.

"That was a real head-banger those two just had. I disagree here and there with Jon but I surely do like his backbone."

"Maybe I'll go talk to him," she said.

"Good idea. Hey, we're just so damn happy you're okay and all. Kate's wanting to help if you need to talk about it."

He gave her shoulder a soft fatherly squeeze and walked back into the hallway toward the living room. Julia hesitated a moment, dropped her attention down into her chest, on down her pelvis and womb, then all the way down in her feet. Walking down the two outside steps and across the side lawn, she came up behind Jon. "Am I intruding?" she asked softly.

He spun around – then relaxed as he took her in. His face was tense. He said nothing.

"I heard that conversation," she confessed.

Jon exhaled loudly through his mouth. "That was so stupid," he muttered. "Waste of time, both of us talking clichés. What makes me mad is I can see his side of all this – that's what Paul was talking about that first day, I was just remembering, it was like I could suddenly hear his voice again, inside my head – weird."

"What were you remembering?" she asked.

"Him saying we have to get beyond all the arguing, focus on what holds us together, not what drives us apart. Sure, that guy scares me, he's dangerous – but Jesus didn't fight and argue, he stayed focused on compassion. That guy in there obviously thinks he's doing good."

"Maybe even the guy who put the bullet in Paul's head thought he was doing good," she said.

"Yeah – Paul was telling us to get beyond the fear, the fighting. Transcend the amygdala – but how? That's exactly the research I want to get into. Strange –– even though Paul's dead and gone I still feel his presence. And I was just remembering – I need to go get all those films that Rupert shot of him, get my hands on the transcripts and TV news footage of everything Paul said and put them in a book or movie or something."

She took two steps and came against him. Their arms held each other softly heart to heart and for a moment there was no flow of words – then Kate's voice was calling them in for dinner.

"But first we've got to catch the guy who shot him. Then I want to head out of this town, quit the Seminary, go down to the ranch for a while – and I know one other thing. I really want you to come with me, if it suits you."

She looked up into his eyes. "Are you sure?"

"Entirely sure."

Julia and Jon were last to sit at the table. Kate served them cheese enchiladas, salad, black beans and Brussel sprouts. Wine glasses were raised. "Here's to all of us being here alive and free," Ty said in his deep voice. "And especially to Julia's heroism. Thank God that's over."

They clinked all around. Julia half-gulped at her wine. Everybody looked down again and gobbled.

"This is real good," Kate told Ty.

"My Gramma," he told her, "brought a solid hit of good ol' Mexican genes into our Hadley blood. And most of that was Oaxacan native."

"Oh?" from Julia.

"Mmm!" from all around.

A satisfied culinary silence befell the group of five around the table. Ty gave everybody time to get well into their enchiladas. Glances flashed around the table but no one spoke up. Julia was nibbling at her food, Jonathan wolfing like he was starving. Kate kept glancing harshly at the federal agent like she expected him to draw his gun any moment.

Then finally Ty put down his fork and turned to the CIA man across the table. "Thomas, I know you need to leave soon, so what is there to discuss – besides whether or not you're the one who shot Paul?"

Thomas raised his head slowly from his plate and looked with cool intent first at Jon, then right at Ty. "You and your kid – you guys are non-stop, I'm surprised you're both not six feet under by now."

"Cowboy habit, call a spade a spade, especially considering your employer's track history plus your general personality and specific behavior."

"Are you actually accusing me of murder?"

"I imagine that if you did it, you're thinking of the deed in much more sanitary CIA terms."

Thomas just sat there a moment, not reacting, looking calmly back at Ty. "Well actually, what you're confessing," he said with just a hint of ingrained professional superiority, "is that you and your female partner actually have zero idea who the murderer is."

"Look me in the eye and answer – did you or one of your trusty helpers shoot Paul Jacobs?"

Thomas put down his fork, leaned back. "No," he said quietly. "We didn't do that."

"So who did, from your high and mighty perspective? Who had the nerve to walk into that room, pick up the .22 pistol that was for some reason just lying around – "

"It happened like I told Kate," Julia spoke up. "Paul had gone down to the dormitories to visit a friend that night, he got drunk and then when he came back, he got delusional or whatever, took on some strange accusatory voice, called me a whore of Babylon or some such, and go t so out of hand that he hit me hard – and so yes, I panicked, went and grabbed the gun from the kitchen drawer and told him to sit down in his chair or I was going to shoot him dead. So sure, he sat, or rather collapsed – and I dropped the pistol on the table and ran out and off to hide. Then it seems somebody came in a few minutes after me, picked up the gun, aimed right at Paul's forehead and fired. Paul was so drunk, he'd probably already passed out – at least I hope so."

There was silence at the table a moment. With glistening eyes, Julia glared at all the eyes looking at her. Then Ty spoke up. "So then, you tell us," he ordered Thomas, "you seem to have spies all over campus – who fired that shot?"

"I have no conclusive evidence. But here's a bit of info. We just got a confession of sorts out of Stuart Wilson at the hospital, he's now revived enough to claim that Douglas McFerrin admitted to him that he was the one who shot Reggie Davis down in cold blood in San Francisco."

"But wait," Julia blurted out, "Douglas told me up at his hideout that he was working for you, so – "

"You didn't mention that at the station."

"You didn't ask," she retorted.

"So tell me what he said."

"Thomas," Kate interrupted, "is that true – was Douglas working for the CIA?"

"He was never mine directly, but yes, sort of – and then he obviously went rogue. We're pleased to have him closed down – but he didn't kill Paul because we know he happened to be socializing with five fellow students in his dorm when Paul was shot."

"Then what about Stuart?" Kate pushed him. "His alibi is virtually non-existent, he could have easily gone up and done it."

"Actually, right at the time of the murder, my sources have documented that Stuart was over in San Rafael at a secret meeting with a group of radicals we also have under surveillance – so to be quite honest, Jonathan here still looks like he did it, based purely on the evidence."

"Bull to that," from Ty.

"Also what you don't know is that the local female minister who killed herself, she was also somewhat involved with our information-gathering. And seeing as how she's dead, a decision has just come down – Wilma's the one we've decided should take the fall for Paul's death. I'm here now to help that process along. She had motive, means and opportunity. I'm offering you all the easy way out."

"Which is exactly?' Kate insisted.

"We together conclude formally that Wilma most likely did the deed. I provide a witness that she was seen up near Paul's cottage. She's got that tell-tail limp. Thus we clear Jon here, erase the kidnapping charges against Douglas, erase Stuart's comment on who shot Reggie. And I take Douglas McFerrin permanently away. The whole situation gets closed, Jonathan here goes free, and I avoid public hearings that would muddle important agency affairs."

"But that stinks," Ty told him bluntly.

"Otherwise after dessert I'm arresting your son as a terrorist and murderer – if you're dumb enough to go against my plan, we all lose. Go my way and everybody wins except a dead woman. So – are we agreed? I need to hit the road."

A phone was ringing somewhere. "That'll be the station," Kate said, walking fast into the next room.

"Like I said," Ty said at Thomas, "your lack of due process stinks to high heaven."

Julia stood abruptly from the table facing Thomas. "Some maniac murdered Paul and you're negotiating like this is a business deal," she shouted at him. "Obviously I want Jon free but I also want whoever killed Paul locked away forever."

"Well sometimes we can't have our cake and eat it too. Let this play out my way – or you lose your lover."

Kate had returned, standing at the doorway. "That was Nora, the professor's wife, and she urgently wants our two youngsters up at the Rosenblum house, it's just five blocks from here, 207 Holsey Drive – up our road half a mile, then take a right. House is on the left. She says the professor is weak but he insists on talking to Jon and Julia. Hopefully he'll shed light on all this."

Immediately Ty was on his feet, Jon and Julia following suit. Thomas was now also standing up. "Wait," he said. "This is Agency work, I'll go up myself and talk to him."

He got three steps toward the front door and then noticed Kate was now holding her police .38 magnum aimed purposefully in the direction of his tight-muscled gut.

"You're not going anywhere."

"Are you kidding?" he retorted.

"She didn't ask for you. And if I shoot somebody prowling in my home here, what with me all anxious that a murderer is still on the loose – that'll be self defense in any court. Who knows, maybe I'd be eliminating the real murderer in the process."

"You don't have the guts to kill anybody," he challenged her.

"You'd be number five," she informed him. "Now you three," she said, waving the pistol at Jon, Julia and Tyson, "you head off and see what's up."

They were fast out the door. "You hold me at gunpoint one more minute," Thomas threatened her, "and I'll make sure you permanently lose your police badge."

It was her turn to smile. "I've already resigned, this is my last day on the job."

"But those three are probably walking right into a trap – the whole thing smells fishy, we both need to get up there and cover their asses."

"You smell more fishy than anything up at the Professor's – you're staying right here till they get back."

"What if they don't come back?"

"Oh," she told him, "I'll probably get so upset that I'll lose my female cool entirely and release my out-of-control emotions on your dead body."

"And go to prison for life."

"Like I said, purely self defense."

32

Night-time had fully engulfed the foothills. The cab of the pickup smelled like Ty's pickups always did – grease and gasoline, tick dip and branding iron, cowboy sweat and sage brush and all the rest. Julia climbed aboard ahead of Jonathan and he settled in beside her, closing the squeaky passenger door. The sounds were soothingly familiar to him, a rattle here and a squeak there as his dad started up and they took off, the Ford engine running a bit rough.

"Who knows best how to get there?" Ty asked as he headed uphill.

"I've been to their house," Julia offered, sitting shoulder to shoulder with the two men in a Hadley sandwich. They rumbled along for a few breaths. Jon put his hand on her knee and heard her exhale softly and settle against him.

"So," he said. "The three Musketeers ride again. Hey Dad, I should probably say sorry for that fake imbibing in the woods."

"Just don't do that again."

"I wanted to blow that guy's mind – did you really think I'd really chug all that acid?"

"What else was I to think?"

"It was so obvious even Thomas caught on."

"So there never were any quarts of LSD?"

"Well I didn't say exactly that."

"I agree with Thomas, that stuff is a hundred percent bad news," Ty grumbled. "But okay, I'm open to evidence regarding Alan's other hundred percent."

"So you talked to Alan?"

"He's not a bad sort. Accepted my invite to come down to the ranch for a visit. Nothing wrong with him that a few days digging post holes won't straighten out."

"Turn here," Julia said.

They drove up a fairly steep hill with towering dark trees on either side of the secluded street. "Slow down – that's their house."

Ty pulled to the curb, cut the engine. In front of the house was a brand new Buick. Inside the dark garage was another vehicle that Ty couldn't quite make out. "You two go in," he told them. "If you need me just shout. Find out what the Professor knows and then let's get back to Kate. Watch your step, I'll cover your back."

"Against what?"

"Who knows, maybe the whole leapin' Judeo-Christian tradition for all I know."

The two of them went up the front steps of the old two-story house. Jonathon pushed the buzzer. There was just one street light, quite a ways down the street from them, but the moon was higher now so they could look back down to where Ty was standing there leaning against the side of the pickup doing nothing – just watching.

"This feels strange here," Jon said. "Dad's got something bugging him related to this house."

"Maybe you didn't hear – we had the Professor and Norrie over to dinner in your cottage last night," Julia told him. "Bernie said he knew something about

Paul's murder – but all he told us was he felt responsible for Paul going crazy because Paul watched him over and over turn into a Prophet, then Paul went and did the same – but as Jesus."

The front door opened. Nora seemed shorter than ever, standing there in some ancient formless old-lady dress. Her expression looked totally crashed, she couldn't even muster her trademark welcoming smile, just stood there staring not quite at anything. Julia walked into the foyer and took the chubby old speechless lady in her arms. then guided her into a cozy living room stuffed with curious antiques and artifacts from the near east. The two women sat down on the sofa. Nora mumbled something Jon couldn't decipher, then burst into tears. Julia raised her head, looked toward the hallway and stairs and nodded slightly for Jonathan to go find the professor.

The house was too quiet, not even a proverbial grandfather clock ticking away the moments. The old man must be somewhere in the house – but maybe there was someone else here as well. Why was Ty so tense, on the look-out? Why was Nora so choked up she couldn't even tell them what was happening?

Just as he entered the downstairs hallway, he realized this could be a set-up, maybe somebody real nasty had forced Nora to phone and beg Jon and Julia to come up here. Reggie's toughs from over in Oakland, or maybe Paul's from back east – very possibly this was all about the LSD. Maybe everything bad that had happened was because Jon had taken that stuff from the Institute – he'd been so angry, wanting to destroy the whole place, set it on fire or something. Instead he'd taken Humphry's chemical A-bomb.

He paused halfway down the dark hallway. Total silence except for Nora still sobbing off in the living room – he wished like hell that Ty with his pistol was beside him. There were two bedroom doors, one right and the other left, both open, both with low lighting as if from reading lamps shining out into the dark hallway. His first impulse was to run back into the living room, grab Julia and get her out the front door down to the pickup. But if there was somebody dangerous in this house, they could leap out to stop him, perhaps get Julia hurt or shot in the process.

He stood there not moving at all, just listening and breathing. "Please God," he found himself silently praying. "Help me out here."

He exhaled slowly, walked forward dizzy with apprehension, turned right at the first bedroom door and saw just what he expected to see – an empty old-fashioned fluffy-lace bed, small antique table and writing chair, dark-wood dresser and a door into a bathroom. There was also a window, the old kind that slides up to let the air in. It was open – wide open.

Something suddenly creaked behind him, up somewhere in the house – were those footsteps? Jon's internal fear center suddenly went on red-alert. It was insane to be in here without a gun. Impulsively deciding he had to get outside to Ty and grab some fire-power, he moved fast across the bedroom, dove right out through the window and fell down hard onto a side lawn.

Unaware of all this, Julia was making little progress with Nora, who was still not speaking. Julia kept looking up for Jonathan to come back or to speak up in the interior of the house – but still no Jon. Perhaps the old man had died. "Nora, all's going to be okay," she said soothingly,

"I'll stay with you tonight and help, do you want me to make us some tea?"

"Oh – yes, yes," she managed to mumble.

"Okay, I'll just be a minute or two."

She left the old woman and headed off into the kitchen. What was that sound – was somebody outside? But no further sounds emerged. Dead silent. She felt her heart accelerating as she walked across the linoleum floor of the kitchen, her steps sounding loud. She made it to the door that, from the kitchen, led either up the stairs or down the hallway where she'd seen Jon disappear a couple of minutes earlier.

"Jon?" she said quietly into the musty air.

No answer.

Walking down the hallway as silently as she could, she looked into the first bedroom on the right – an open window, nothing else. She walked to the door on the left, went in two steps and came to a stop. There was the old man in a high four-poster bed, lying on his back, his great nose still prominent even in his life-weakened state. She glanced fast around the room. No Jon.

"Professor?" she half-whispered. No answer. He was either asleep or in a coma, or dead – she didn't quite know which and right then she didn't want to do any experiments to find out. Instead she turned and walked quickly through the other rooms downstairs, then headed up the stairs. Somehow Jon had totally disappeared. Her impulse was to take off out the front door and get Ty – but she feared that if something weird was happening here, something weird enough to make Jon disappear, then if she bolted and ran, who knows what would happen to Jon and Nora.

She headed instead back down the creaky stairs. "Norrie," Julia whispered as she came into the living room, "Jon's just – disappeared somewhere. Is there anyone in the house?"

The old lady, sitting a bit more upright now, met her eyes vaguely. "Well – yes."

"Tell me who and where – now!"

"The bedroom on your right, like I said."

"How many people?"

"Oh – just the one."

"Well one's one too many. I want you to get up with me right now and walk as quickly as you can to the front door and right on outside."

But at just that moment the front door banged open and in rushed two wild men waving firearms and shouting. Both Julia and Nora sat back down on the sofa as if hit by the attacking energy of invaders.

Ty swung around to Jon who was standing beside him with a .45 pistol in hand. "So we take each room together – move!"

They disappeared on the run. The women just sat. "Are those men crazy?" Nora whispered to Julia, who was sitting there listening to the pounding of male boot heels heading up the stairs.

Jonathan was panting like crazy, so was his father as they moved fast, room by room, expecting at any moment to run into lethal fire. But in the end they seemed to be running around in circles, finally pausing for breath up in a steep-roofed attic where a solitary ancient light bulb swung eerily between them.

"Fuck," from Ty.

"False alarm – sorry," from Jon.

"You drive me crazy, kid."

"Wait – what was that sound?"

"Quick – downstairs!"

And so they went running down the stairs of the old house and came storming into the living room a second time in five minutes. The two women again looked up at them – but this time the look on the women's faces was exasperation.

"What in hell are you doing?" Julia insisted.

Jon came to a full stop just three feet from her, looking fast around the room. Ty did the father version of same. Then and only then did both of them finally realize something at the same time – and then glance at each other.

"Are you crazy?" Julia said hotly. "There's an old man dying in this house and you're acting like it's cops and robbers."

"But – I thought," Jon started.

"I just now got my flashlight out and found the '56 blue Chevy in the garage," Ty spoke up, "so we assumed – but it looks like we were wrong. Unless there's still somebody out there somewhere."

Jonathan made a fast move, went to the window and peered out at the moonlit street.

"All clear out there," he said.

"But the Chevy?" Ty asked.

"Oh, we've had that all these years since we moved out here," Norrie told him.

Ty got the point, shook his head, walked over and sat down heavily on a chair. "Damn. I'm too old for this," he said. "I'd rather hunt down rustlers."

"Jonathan," Julia said to her lover's back.

"Yeah, well," Jon said, finally making his about-face. "Uhm. Sorry about all that. I panicked. Been a long day. Very long. For you too."

"Nora," Ty said to the old woman. "We found Bernie in there in his bed. Has he actually, uhm, has he passed on?"

"Oh yes, he said his final goodbye to me half an hour ago," Nora reported, seeming in full awake-mode finally. "He's almost certainly gone this time but who knows, he's said goodbye several time before. That man had a most advanced flair for drama. He would have been an actor but in old-time Germany when we met, Jews were no longer allowed to act on stage. Back then all the laws of the land became more and more strange until in the end, all we had to hold onto were the laws in the bible. That's how Bernie kept his sanity – he held onto the laws of the Old Testament, and then yes, he discovered the higher laws of Jesus. And now, assuming he doesn't start breathing again, he's finally free of laws altogether. Or maybe there are laws in heaven – if so, then count me out. Sorry Bernie, I might not join you ... this might really be goodbye."

Tears welled in her already well-teared eyes.

"Here," Julia offered, handing her a tissue.

"Ah, thank you dearie. You're just the sweetest thing, and that man of yours is the luckiest in the world – but he's perhaps not quite right in the head, running around with that pistol. I say, put it down, never leave pistols around where children and old men might find them. Oh Julia, I can't even bring myself to tell you."

"Tell me what?"

"Bernie made me promise with a solemn vow – he confessed to me just an hour ago, as his breaths became more and more shallow – oh I must tell you quick and get back to his side. He was such a dynamo in his younger days, but age does sometimes take away all the marbles."

She stopped talking, stared with luminous eyes into blank space – then came back into her body with a very slight shiver from toes to head.

Jon glanced from the old woman to the pistol in his hand, then looked directly over at Julia who at that moment was looking directly at him. Ty watched them, saw their intensity, their mutual vulnerability – and his heart suddenly ached so much in his chest that he thought the pain might be the beginning of a heart attack, he had just too much pain deep in his heart ... but then his eyes looked over and found Julia looking intently his way with a slight smile – and he felt something right in the very middle of his being suddenly relax ...

Jonathan meanwhile put the pistol down on the coffee table and nodded to Nora as if wanting her to continue talking, and she did: "Bernie would not have let you be convicted of shooting Paul," she told him. "He loved you, he loved all his students and he loved Paul the most, God bless both of them. He would tell me after class that Paul was the one he'd been waiting for, the chosen one to replace him in his work. He told me that Paul was touched with greatness, that he understood. And then oh God damn him, he went and shot him."

The room became engulfed in breathless silence. Three pairs of eyes stared at the fourth pair – and the fourth pair had the gumption to turn and look at each of the other three pairs in turn before she commenced talking. "Imagine – my very own man – how can I live on? But both Bernie and Paul taught that Jesus told us not to judge God's creation, and surely they were right. So who am I to judge Bernie and you must understand, it wasn't even Bernie at that moment he fired the pistol, it was Elijah or Joshua or – I can't keep them all straight, I loved the man but I didn't care for his theology. But oh, those prophets of old, they were so very good in bed. Oops, did I say that out loud – I wouldn't want to read any of this in the papers if you can help it. I'll be moving out of this house anyway, this was his dream home, not mine. It's all about love though, isn't it? Anyway Bernie's confession was very simple as he told it. He was coming home from the administration meeting that night, he'd driven down himself even though I told him I'd drive him – there were many times when he was impossible but now I'm somehow feeling guilty for Paul's death because I didn't resist more and drive him myself."

"There's no guilt, Norrie," Julia said softly.

"Well Bernie drove away from the administration building headed home but instead he drove up the hill to the path that goes to the married cottages. He told me Spirit told him to go to Paul and free him from his Jesus possession – so he made his way up that trail using his walking stick I'm sure although he didn't mention that. He told me he found Paul drunk and hostile and claiming that he was in fact not Jesus Christ incarnate but rather Lucifer himself, taking over the world in the body of this man named Paul. You can imagine – this claim was so outrageously blasphemous that Bernie suddenly snapped into one of his transcendent raging old-time prophets of the Lord who saw before him the ultimate evil force of the universe – and so yes, Bernie grabbed a stray pistol laying right there on Paul's coffee table and ordered that demon to come out of Paul."

She stopped talking, her mouth hanging open as she stared out the window for two gasping breaths ... and then she continued: "I'm not sure what else happened at that point, what Paul might have said back to him – for you see, Bernie had started mumbling to me in some foreign language, his beloved Hebrew I think it was, saying things I didn't understand at all – but obviously for Bernie the demon refused to come out and so the Lord's prophet carried through with exactly what he'd threatened. Acting as the righteous hand of God, Bernie killed that demon bang – dead."

She seemed finished. Julia was staring at her, not quite able to process what she'd just heard. Ty cleared his throat and said softly, "Nora, please – did Bernie say anything more?"

She suddenly stood up. "I must go to him ... but now that I think about it, yes indeed, I recall the very last thing Bernie said to me in English, bless his heart. He said that he could see now quite clearly that he hadn't managed to kill the demon after all – he'd somehow shot an angel instead."

~~~~~~~~~~~~~~~~~~~

John Selby ~ Author Note

As some of you might know, my non-fiction books and meditation apps and videos and all the rest focus strongly on how to let go of the past and live more mindfully in the here-and-now. So why have I written this historical novel, based on events I lived through forty-some years ago?

Well, partly because writing this book has been great fun – but also, it seems that during the last forty years my mind has been busy at mostly unconscious levels transforming personal memory into a more mythic essence of what we struggled through during those seminal late-sixties in America when the visionary foundations of the psych-tech revolution were being forged in youthful minds.

I admit that including real historic people like Alan Watts and several others as characters was at first a bit scary – but I had great fun reviving the lingering essence of historic people, portraying them as I knew them way back then. I certainly mean no malice toward these historic characters – but I also have been at times a bit brutal in portraying the real people as I knew them, not their present-day over-polished images. For instance I knew Alan Watts in real life quite well, first from the Institute and then in Sausalito, and I do like how he comes to life in this story as a complex full human being.

I also want to state here that a real-life seminary friend of mine (perhaps packing a slight schizophrenic edge) did take LSD in January 1969, under my guidance, hoping to explore the outer reaches of his mystic mind. Instead for two weeks this very real person unexpectedly became transformed into a walking-talking modern-day Jesus Christ character, with news crews following him around just as in our story – before suddenly popping out of the spell and returning to quasi-normal. The real Paul haunts me still, and in a way this book is an homage to him and to the core issues he raised during his temporary transformation.

As regards Jonathan and his father Tyson, suffice it to say that I took a number of real people very close to home and played quite freely with them, as any full-blooded fiction author does, in order to create characters who serve the story and at the same time ring true as genuine human beings. Tyson Hadley is a very believable version of my own father, who was a cattle rancher and deputy sheriff just like in the story – but Ty's attitudes and relationship status have been shifted considerably in order to meet the demands of the plot.

And Jonathan – his in-print character will in fact go to Stanford and become the primary professorial instigator of the much-later suspense plots that propel my novels *Google Beta 3* and *Ten % Max*. Getting to know him here helps those later stories about his son Jack Hadley make even more sense. Also for the records, there was indeed a blatant historic theft of several Sandoz LSD bottles from

Humphrey Osmond's research institute where I had worked back east. The devious and at times nasty CIA agent looking for the thief in this story is modeled on a real live government guy who hounded me seriously back then. For legal reasons, I still have no comment about who stole those bottles, nor what was done with their contents.

The San Francisco Theological Seminary is drawn fairly accurately from the still-existing religious institution, although the campus is now more conservative than it was back then. I did take major liberty in the fictional characters related to the Seminary – especially the president: the real-life president at that time was a most wonderful person, quite different from the one in this book.

The backdrop of the Vietnam war and the revolutionary '60s situations in San Francisco and Berkeley are drawn from history as I lived through it. The New Jersey Neuropsychiatric Institute's Experimental Psychology Section (with its secret MK-Ultra funding and intent) did send me as an observer during the summer of 1967 to Haight-Ashbury, where I innocently wrote weekly letters describing what I was experiencing.

The driving political and spiritual themes of the day, portrayed as deeply as I could in this police-procedure novel, seem as relevant today as they were forty (or a thousand) years ago. Certainly the issue of otherwise-honest upstanding Americans turning into psych-tech terrorists to fight governmental and societal injustice remains hot and real. When religion mixes with politics and drugs, look out!

Please hold in mind that my novel-writing imagination is far more acrobatic than my memory; this is mostly a work of fiction. By coincidence I'm releasing this historic novel at the same time that I release my two contemporary 'psych-tech suspense' novels, *Google Beta 3* and *Ten % Max*. These two novels take place in our near future and feature Jonathan's son Jack Hadley, who's carrying on after his father has been murdered at Stanford. It's a Google-enmeshed plot dramatically exposing the dangers and possibilities inherent in using technology to alter and control human thought and emotion – our next unavoidable frontier.

These books can be read in any order, with *Shooting Angels* standing as a prequel to the other two novels, or on its own. Right now I'm working on the screenplays for these novels – and also just finished a fourth novel in the series called *Vibe Tribe* following the adventures of Jonathan Hadley's cousin Benjamin Hadley in a 1980's terrorist-bashing escapade in Europe that sheds even more light on the nefarious Institute research.

I'm also in the formative stages of creating a fifth novel in this series called *Mahee Speaks*. Finally Mahalena Bernhardt of *Google Beta 3* is going to get to step forward first-person as she plunges through a hellish situation in northern Afghanistan (written before the recent news of a real-life kidnapping similar to hers) that hopefully sheds new light on how we might finally become a bright post-terrorist world society.

And of final note – after nearly 50 years of writing and rewriting a novel with Paul Davids about what actually happened at the Institute and Princeton, we're pleased to announce that this very first exposé story about that MK-Ultra CIA situation is now complete and heading for publication – and this very first book chronologically, aptly called *Blowing America's Mind*, is entirely grounded in fact. Paul and I had to hypnotize each other over and over, in order to access those memories – and finally we broke through and succeeded. You can read sample chapters of all these interrelated novels online.

For more, please visit my author website:

www.johnselby.com

~~~~~~~~~~~~~~~~

Reading Group Questions
~~~~~~~~~~~~~~~~~

1: *Shooting Angels* merges several different genres into one fast-paced plot. Did you feel comfortable with the juxtaposition of a religious seminary with such issues as psychedelic drugs and murder – or did the author violate long-standing rules about not mixing spirituality and violence, drugs and religion, meditation and sex?

2: The author attended the San Francisco Theological Seminary during this late-sixties time period, and left his ministerial position amid accusations and denouncements from the Presbyterian church. Do you feel he was perhaps seeking a bit of revenge in writing this book, or did he give the seminary and the church a fair shake?

3: Were your own religious and spiritual sensibilities affirmed or violated by this rather raucous sexy secular assault on cherished religious beliefs and institutions? Did reading this novel have any effect on your own beliefs and spiritual assumptions etc?

4: Ty Hadley the cattle-rancher father comes riding into town to defend his son and arrest the real murderer. He loves his son but also holds truth and justice supreme. Was he a believable character for you? The author combined several real-life relatives into this father-figure character. Did the author create a solid American hero?

5: The plot exposes several sides of the ongoing psychedelic controversy – father Ty's serious skepticism, his son's tentative praise for the drug's spiritual impact, plus an exposé of the commercial illegal-drug-market dimension – and also the drug's potential as a radical weapon for social and political change. After reading this book, what are your feelings about the use of LSD and other psychedelic drugs in safe situations for spiritual growth, and its potential to damage to our youth, or perhaps to provoke rapid positive social change?

6: The CIA is presented in a complex way in this book, sometimes with usual stereotypes, sometimes with a deeper look into its agents and their professional and personal intent. After reading this book, what are your feelings about the way the author presented the historical CIA as an organization trying to secretly influence and contain change in our society?

7: Ty's son Jon sometimes appears a bit weak and confused, at other times he's clear and dynamic. Were you pleased with this character, did you warm to him and root for him and feel good about his sexual relationship and final success in the plot, or did you find him violating beliefs you hold close to your heart?

8: The author of this book is mostly a quick-stroke zen-style writer. The book is lean and fast, quickly flowing from one action scene to another without much traditional author reflection and philosophical depth, at least on the surface. Did you enjoy the author's fast pace and style, or were you hungry for more length to the book, so that you could get to know the situation and characters more fully?

9: Alan Watts was a real person whom the author knew quite well – but in *Shooting Angels* the author plays freely with this deceased person, using him to serve the plot rather than delving into his real life. Did you enjoy this touch of historic character in the plot, or do you feel authors don't have the right to use historic characters in this way?

10: At the Monday Night Class in the City portrayed in this book, the charismatic teacher is portraying a real-life person called Steve Gaskin. Did you enjoy and appreciate the several pages of spiritual discussion in that scene, or were you put off by the author's inclusion of this view of spirituality in the book?

11: This is a historic novel, set fifty years in the past. Much has happened since the psychedelic revolution. But again, much remains the same and continues to advance as Baby Boomers who were kids during the 60's now become seniors and continue to influence our society. What are your feelings about the ongoing impact of the wild 60's and 70's on our society – was the injection of psychedelics into our youth culture in the long run positive, or negative?

12: The invention of LSD in 1938 was an early psych-tech creation that continues to impact our world society. Do you think it's a good idea for people to use such potent psychotropic chemicals to stimulate unique experience in their brains and bodies, hearts and souls – or should we avoid all psych-tech tools that are just emerging, and leave our minds alone?

For more on these themes, feel free to read
the author's ongoing blogs and video discussions at:

www.johnselby.com

Enjoy Three More Jack Hadley Mysteries:

GOOGLE BETA 3

TEN % MAX

VIBE TRIBE

and also

BLOWING AMERICA'S MIND

~~~~~~~~~~~~~~~~~